Divinity Undone

HOUSE OF BORGIA

MICHELLE ELLIOTT

MICHELLE ELLIOTT

CHAPTER ONE

Divinity Undone

Lucrezia always referred to her father as "uncle." A term he insisted on. As newly ordained Pope Alexander VI, Lucrezia was still his bastard daughter and had little choice but to obey. Before the great anointing, Rodrigo Borgia flaunted power and ambition as an influential Cardinal with a mistress and many illegitimate children. As the Holy Father of all Christendom, Rodrigo set the rules. He demanded loyalty and obedience from everyone - even God himself.

Lucrezia cared little what title the man held or what she called him, admiring the full-length mirror sent as a present from her father, the new Pope. Her recently appointed apartment lay on the east side of the apostolic palace, far from political affairs and church business. The second-floor chamber window offered a sweeping view of the countryside and the beautiful garden courtyard below.

The display of Vatican wealth was breathtaking, even though her life had been far from penniless. Ornate gold leaf covered the wall paneling, and the vaulted ceiling portrayed a brightly painted mural of St. Anne, the patroness of unmarried women. Besides several clothing coffers that lined the wall, other rooms as large as her bedchamber were dedicated solely to her royal wardrobe.

Lucrezia pulled a dress from the pile on the bed and studied the elaborate satin design and low-cut bodice. In her fourteenth year, her body had finally matured. The sleek curve of her hips had taken shape, accentuating her petite waist. Childhood plumpness had been replaced with elegant cheekbones and a smooth stomach, but her breasts remained no larger than two firm peaches. She frowned. Would her bosom even fill any gown? She placed the elaborate hairpiece on her head. The weight crushed her golden ringlets as the words "Lady of Procida" repeated hypnotically in her mind. Uncle Rodrigo had made good on his promise of betrothal. It was one of the first papal decrees he made after becoming Pope Alexander. This evening, a formal dinner was planned to meet her fiancé, Don Gaspare Aversa, a young Procida nobleman. That was all she had been told of the boy who was to be her husband. It was all quite unfair, in her opinion.

"You primp like a peacock, Lucrezia," Giulia teased and rubbed her swollen pregnant belly.

"And you are a jealous hag," she countered and ducked as a hairbrush barely missed her head.

Giulia's temper was legendary. As her uncle's mistress, Giulia Farnese had Rodrigo's ear, shared his bed, and flaunted his extravagant gifts, but she lacked the one thing she wanted most. The girl would never be his wife. As much as Giulia denied it, everyone suffered the prospect of her remaining his eternal mistress. Only five years Lucrezia's senior, Giulia treated her like a daughter, telling Lucrezia what fabric to choose for new gowns, how to hold a spoon, and what fruits to eat to keep a smooth, firm stomach.

Giulia's own belly bulged like a full barrel. Privately, the announcement of her pregnancy had pleased Rodrigo. His virility was one thing he valued as much as becoming pontiff. Publicly, the news brought a cool indifference from Rodrigo, which infuriated Giulia. She was already married to a noble crusader. Yet, to no one's dismay, Rodrigo sent the man away a year ago to fight a long, drawn-out crusade in Turkey. Giulia did not care. If becoming Rodrigo's wife was impossible, even with an unconstrained husband, at the very least, she would bear Rodrigo children.

Lucrezia pulled up her long golden hair and twisted it away from her face, trying to decide how to best wear it for the upcoming feast. "What does Don Gaspare look like?" she asked, in an effort towards reconciliation, aware that Giulia had already glimpsed her fiancé that morning at Mass.

"He is a pompous ass masquerading as someone important when he is only a boy of sixteen!" she answered, her voice still sharp.

Lucrezia let her hair fall and flopped down on the bed, sprawling across the mountain of gowns. "Giulia, you know what I mean. What color is his hair? His eyes? Is he thin? Short? What about his face? Is it kind?" Even though Lucrezia did not know these things, she was sure she loved him already. Besides her brothers, Juan, Cesare, and Gioffre, she had never spent much time in the company of other boys but dreamt of them often.

Giulia's eyes softened. "He is slightly taller than you. His hair is brown, the color of wheat berries in October. He is slight of build and immature... rather silly for my taste." She threw a comb at Lucrezia but playfully this time. "I spoil you."

"My husband will spoil me," Lucrezia answered, sure of the future. "He will love only me, and I will bear him many children."

Giulia tossed back her head and laughed. "Sweet child, love has nothing to do with it! You must learn how to please a man to keep him."

Lucrezia's mother, the beautiful and formidable Vannozza, had never discussed such things. When told Lucrezia was to live at the palace with her father and older brothers, Vannozza cursed Rodrigo for taking away her children, especially Lucrezia, who was still young and impressionable. In bed each night, when the extravagance and whirlwind of palace life faded and her unsettled mind reflected on the uncertain future, she longed for her mother.

Lucrezia had lived within the Vatican walls now for almost four months in the charge of Giulia and the governess, Adriana. Her mother's absence left no means to garner the knowledge needed to navigate the adult world, except for Giulia, who not only shimmered with sexual prowess but appeared eager to impart such expertise. At night, the palace hummed with life. The murmurs and contented sighs behind her uncle's chamber door occupied Lucrezia's time late at night. With her ear pressed against the heavy wood, images of what could cause such ecstasy were endless.

"You must learn the power of seduction," Giulia explained, "then the art of lovemaking."

"That is impossible, locked behind the palace walls, never seeing the world!"

"You hear enough slinking around the Vatican halls at night," Giulia shot back with a raised eyebrow, aware of Lucrezia's late-night sleuthing.

The Pope's mistress sat on the bed and grasped Lucrezia's hands, her face solemn. "This much you must know. The man thrusts his cock inside your cunny for pleasure. Sometimes the result is a baby," she stated bluntly.

"My uncle did that to you!" Lucrezia exclaimed, horrified.

Giulia laughed. "Many times. The pleasure is great once you teach a man how to please you."

"Tell me!" she begged. "You must tell me everything!"

Suddenly, the door flung open, and Adriana, returning from her daily novena, rushed into the bedchamber. The heavy cross around her neck was a constant reminder of her duty to the Pope to keep his daughter obedient and chaste and protect her from the sin of lust.

"I see you have yet to choose a gown," the older woman snapped. Her thin, squinty face scowled at Giulia. "And you have been no help."

"Offering the finer points regarding the marital bed is always useful. Am I right, Lucrezia?" Giulia winked and giggled, watching the color rise in Lucrezia's cheeks.

"Be gone!" Adriana shooed Giulia off the bed and towards the door. "The child's head need not be filled with such debauchery."

Giulia stopped just as Adriana prepared to slam the door behind her. "Be mindful of to whom you speak, old woman." Giulia's hands rested comfortably on her belly.

Adriana's flinty glare never wavered, but instead of a dramatic slam, the door closed softly behind the Pope's mistress, and she turned her attention back to the gowns. Adriania snatched a dress from the pile. "This will do. Now come with me. We need to find slippers and jewels. There is no time for indecision."

Lucrezia's mouth opened but stopped short. Adriana was correct. The afternoon had nearly passed, and it would take hours to get ready. Besides, the gown's deep indigo velvet and silver embroidery complimented Lucrezia's fair complexion. Her future husband would appreciate her beauty and charm. He would laugh at her quick wit and marvel at her fluent Latin, Greek, and French. He would fall hopelessly in love with her. Everything would be perfect.

***

Rain poured from the purplish sky like sins purged from heaven. The banquet guests seated in the great hall were deaf to the fat raindrops that plopped down on the terracotta roof. Still, Lucrezia had seen the menacing storm clouds gather from her window overlooking one of the many apostolic gardens. Just as the storm overtook the palace, Adriana whisked her away to the banquet to meet her fiancé, her first true love. Now, in an outer room, Lucrezia sat nibbling her fingernails, waiting to be announced.

"Stop fidgeting!" Adriana swatted her hand.

As Rodrigo's cousin, Adriana took her position as governess seriously. Unfortunately, the position lacked warmth and sentimentality, making Lucrezia long for her mother. The one person who calmed her fears kissed her face and told her how beautiful she looked and how fortunate any man would be to have her hand in marriage. Instead, Lucrezia had to withstand Adriana's scrutiny and endless prodding like a cow prepared for the market.

"It is time." Johann Burchard, the Pope's loyal secretary, stood before her, hands folded as if in prayer, his formal robes befitting the master of ceremony. His olive-colored face was grave, and behind his austerity hid a disdain for her gender, a contempt at the responsibility of managing a female in the apostolic palace.

Burchard lightly held Lucrezia's elbow as she proceeded at a slow, formal gait. Adriana fell behind while the enormous doors that led to the grand banquet hall closed in their wake. Lucrezia's eyes drifted to the arched ceiling above the dinner guests. Lively frescoes and priceless paintings in massive gold frames adorned the walls. The table was long and laden with platters of rice puddings, ox and venison, grapes, cheese, and bread. Silver pitchers flowed with fine wine and mead. She had spied on grand banquets before, as her uncle had held many dinners over the past several weeks to thank his election supporters, but the flickering candles and flashes of gold tumblers were still breathtaking. As the guest of honor, her head swirled with nerves and anticipation.

Borgia and Aversa families sat across from each other, her uncle at the head of the table. Rodrigo smiled warmly at her and nodded at a vacant chair near him. His pale blue tiara sat grandly on his head like an enormous, exquisitely decorated egg. His stern face, with its deep fragmented lines, revealed the difficult, even dangerous, struggle he had endured to become Pope Alexander VI.

Gracefully, Lucrezia settled in to dine, aware of the stares and silent assessments. Juan and Cesare, her older brothers, sat beside her, along with a few of her uncle's loyal Cardinals. Juan's eyes were already red and glassy from the potent wine. Across sat her future father-in-law, a large man with a puffy face and thick neck.

Lucrezia lifted her eyes and peered at the delegation across the table. Halfway down was a slightly older boy. His tawny curls touched his shoulders, and his face illuminated with good humor at the lively conversation of perhaps an older uncle beside him. He raised his wine glass as if to toast and drank deeply. He accepted more wine from a servant and glanced at the table after catching her gaze. The pleasant smile vanished, and he looked away.

"Lucrezia, eat something." Cesare placed a hunk of cheese on her plate and filled her goblet with wine.

She nodded at the boy. "Who is he?"

Cesare laughed. "That, good Sister, is your future husband. The man who will make you a lady and help us gain important allies."

"He does not care for me," she said, pouting into her wine.

"Don't be a fool. We have not even introduced you."

"He does not look at me. Am I not beautiful?"

A thin yet firm hand suddenly covered her small hand completely. "You are as beautiful as an angel," the Pope interrupted. "A delight for the eyes. Sent by God himself."

Her wan smile was not convincing. If this boy wanted to be her husband, he needed to behave better than an aloof dinner guest.

Rodrigo motioned at the lute and tabor players eager to entertain. "A song so that the young couple may dance!"

The man with the puffy face nodded his approval as the musicians waited for the couple.

Perspiration gathered above her lip. Dancing with this stranger was not her intent, especially in front of gawking men. She remained seated and prayed for a distraction, a deliverance, or any disruption to save her from the uncomfortable circumstance. From under the table, a stiff boot kicked her calf. Her eyes met Juan's grave stare.

"Do it!" he seethed and pinched her arm for added incentive.

Unable to escape, Lucrezia made her way to the dance floor, the skin on her arm still pulsing from Juan's pinch. Don Gaspare already waited in the open space dedicated to dance and revelry. He was well-dressed, with an athletic build, not much taller than her. Lucrezia held up her hands and searched the dull eyes of her would-be husband, hopeful for a flicker of mutual attraction. Instead, he took her trembling fingers and stared straight ahead, slightly over her forehead, avoiding her gaze. The "tap, tap, tap" told them what beat to expect. As the strumming began, her right foot moved forward to start the quick-paced balletti. Unfortunately, Don Gaspare was a half-step behind. Lucrezia stepped on his boot, and the precisely orchestrated dance was ruined.

He pushed her away and hopped on one foot, feigning pain. "Do you not know how to dance? Have you not been properly trained?"

The table of men roared with laughter. Tears burned her eyes. Lucrezia's dance training was impeccable. Antonio Vasquez, her teacher, said so many times. She danced the balletti perfectly, even without music. So why was this boy willing to humiliate her in front of everyone? She looked to her uncle to save her, but even he joined Don Gaspare's father in hearty laughter.

"Your foot was out of step! You are a clumsy fool who does not know the simple balletti!" she answered with venom.

The men laughed harder when Juan called out, "Ah, the couple's first argument!"

Lucrezia gathered her skirts and rushed from the room. Burchard called from behind, commanding her to stop, but she could not. Tears streamed down her face as she raced through the palace until she reached the safety of her bedchamber.

"What is wrong, child?" Adriana asked accusingly when Lucrezia burst into the room and flung herself onto the bed.

"Don Gaspare is a beast! I never want to see him again!"

Giulia slipped into the room and whispered to Adriana, who clucked her tongue and busied herself with a coffer of clothes.

"You will see him again, and soon. Your uncle will not be pleased if you do not make amends," Giulia told her.

"Never!" she shouted and buried her face in her hands, rouge smeared across her face. "Don Gaspare ruined the dance! He is the one who should apologize!"

Giulia sat down and pulled Lucrezia's hands from her face. "The marriage will take place whether you like it or not," she said sternly. "Don Gaspare Aversa will be your husband, and you will be Lady of Procida."

"I will talk to my uncle."

"It will do no good."

"He loves me and wants what is best for me."

Giulia stood and planted her hands on her once narrow hips. "He wants what is good for the Borgias. He wants what is good for him. The sooner you accept that, the happier you will be."

***

The bright morning sun made the pear and cherry trees glisten from the heavy rain the night before. Lucrezia had tossed and turned in the dark, reliving the horrible scene at the banquet. Giulia's words strummed through her dreams like a minstrel's strange and confusing ballad. She doubted Giulia. Her uncle loved her. He wanted her to be happy. But Don Gaspare would never make her happy. She would tell her uncle her decision to end the ill-matched betrothal immediately following morning Mass. She hurried through the garden and across St. Peter's Square to the domed basilica, hoping she was not late.

The Papal Palace and Basilica of St. Peter were busy during the morning hours. The immense stone structure of the cathedral stood as a beacon of Christendom with

its soaring columns and massive statues of St. Peter and
St. Paul gracing the arched entrance. Everyone attended
Mass. Clergy and laymen bustled across the cobbled stones
with the same spiritual diligence. When a hand gripped her
arm, Lucrezia turned, expecting a servant or nun wishing
to accompany her. Instead, it was the grinning face of Don
Gaspare.

"What are you doing?" she seethed under her breath.

"Escorting my future wife to Mass," he replied, his dark
eyes wide with amusement.

"We are not to be alone."

He glanced around, his curls covered with a hood.
"How can we be alone amongst all these people? Are you
blind?"

"Again, you insult me."

"A joke. A foolish joke," he blurted. "I am sorry."

She did not answer, unsatisfied by his half-hearted
apology. Even in a crowd, they needed to be properly
chaperoned. Although he might not care, she refused to
have her reputation sullied.

"Unhand me, or I'll scream," she warned.

"I need to speak to you. Alone." He squeezed her arm
more firmly. "All alone."

The urgency in his voice intrigued her. Why was he
so willing to face severe admonishment for ignoring
courtship etiquette?

"Please," he said, more heartfelt this time. "No harm will come to you."

She stopped, and the crowd parted around them like two stones in a stream. His large, serious eyes locked onto hers, revealing a maturity she had not noticed before.

"Very well."

They worked their way through the crowd, turning back to the gardens. The south garden was large and open, but pathways led to smaller, more secluded yards meant for quiet reflection and prayer.

"Follow me," she said. She held out her palm, and Don Gaspare's hand slid into hers like a glove of the finest doeskin. A flicker of desire rose below her stomach.

They reached a small garden filled with red and yellow rose bushes. A bronze statue of St. Francis stood in the corner, and a delicate lily pond dotted the center. She led him to a bench made of stone slab and, reluctantly, released his soft hand. Silence engulfed the sweet morning air.

"My governess will punish me for missing Mass," she finally said, unable to stand the quiet any longer.

"It is beautiful here," he said, ignoring her concern. He removed his hood and took in the manicured hedges and robust flowers. "Procida is beautiful too, but different. Great cliffs circle my country like a rugged necklace. The sea surrounding the island is such a magnificent cobalt blue, a color blue I thought could exist nowhere else." He

caught her face between his hands, and her eyes widened.
"Until now."

Her cheeks burned, and his gaze touched her
somewhere inside, making her want to kiss his tender lips.
Her eyes closed, and his mouth pressed against hers. His
tongue parted her lips and gently explored her mouth,
darting back and forth against the soft inner lining. His
mouth moved to her ear and nibbled the lobe before
moving down her neck, then to her breasts that heaved,
begging to be released.

"Stop!" Burchard stood under the garden archway.

Her heart ceased. Don Gaspare pulled away, and she
sprang to her feet. Her shame glowed red on her cheeks.

"We were kissing," she stammered, unable to meet
Burchard's glare, "just kissing."

"I saw what you were doing," he answered, hurrying
across the lawn.

"My sincere apology," Don Gaspare called out
sheepishly.

The man, noted to be her uncle's trusted advisor, took
three daunting steps toward her fiancé. Burchard was
slender yet broad through the shoulders and, with his
apostolic hat, towered over Don Gaspare. "Be silent! You
dare risk Lady Lucrezia's reputation with your deception
and arrogance?"

"Please don't tell my uncle!" Lucrezia pleaded, having
witnessed the man's wrath before.

Burchard pointed a crooked finger at her fiancé. "Go to the Basilica. Find your people." He turned and pointed the same finger at her. "You go, too. Find Giulia and Adriana. Pray hard that my memory fails me when asked why you were both late for Mass!"

Chapter Two

"Your mind drifts like a lily on water," Sister Angelina scolded. "You waste my time. I pray you return for evening prayers with restored motivation."

Lucrezia nodded, relieved that the old nun appreciated the pointlessness of the day's Latin translation. She snapped the primer shut, glad to be done. The late afternoon sun waned in the hazy sky as she left the little chapel and hurried back to her apartments. Pietra, her newly appointed maid, hastened behind. After the incident in the garden, Lucrezia was never alone. Even while using the privy, Pietra dutifully waited outside. She was sure someone guarded her bedchamber door at night, maybe even watching as she slept.

Two weeks had passed since the encounter with Don
Gaspare, and something had troubled her ever since. She
glimpsed him briefly, once on his way to wrestle Juan
and then again while riding out on a hunt. Don Gaspare
did not turn to her as she expected, but like a doe
chased by hunters, her heart raced at the sight of him. She
remembered the kiss in the garden as if it had happened
mere seconds ago. It stirred in her a desire for attention
and affection. Never had anyone mentioned the color of
her eyes or compared them to the bluest of oceans. She
prayed her future husband's indifference towards her now
resulted from Burchard's fury and the threat of revealing
their indiscretion to her uncle.

Thoughts of her nuptials consumed her. She had only
attended one wedding, the marriage of her older cousin
Paolina in Florence when she was a child. The flutter of
white doves filled the air, and the clanging of church bells
flooded the streets. The magnificent feast lasted all night.
She remembered throwing a tantrum for being sent to bed
early. Paolina's wedding would never compare to her own.
Her wedding would have twice as many doves and ringing
bells, and the festivities would go on as long as she and
her beloved Don Gaspare wanted before he took her to his
bed.

Back at the apartment, Pietra closed the bedchamber
door behind them, and Lucrezia gasped. Burchard and
her uncle, the Pope, were seated by the garden window,

speaking in inaudible whispers. Someone had closed the large metal shutters and laid fruit and cheese on the sideboard. Their conversation ceased, and both faces turned to her and brightened in a sly, knowing way. Her uncle rarely visited her apartments since their move to the apostolic palace. Burchard alone usually did his bidding.

"Wait outside," Burchard told Pietra, and the girl dipped into a deep curtsy and disappeared.

Her uncle smiled and beckoned her to come closer. Dressed in a simple mozzetta draped over his ashen papal robe, the lack of color made his skin appear gray and pallid. Lucrezia approached the men, curtsied, and kissed the newly cast signet ring on her uncle's outstretched hand. The cold metal held his distinguished profile, including his prominent Spanish nose and pursed disapproving lips. Her pulse quickened with the thought that the wedding date was finally at hand. Dowry negotiations completed. Alliances made. Why else would her uncle be in her apartment?

"You are well?" her uncle asked, sounding more like a statement.

"Very well," she answered.

He motioned for her to sit.

A stack of papers sat on Burchard's lap. He studied the parchments earnestly as if to remove himself from the impending conversation.

Her uncle folded his hands on his lap. "I am here regarding your marriage."

Her cheeks flushed. She was certain the men could hear her heart pound.

"I have annulled the arrangement," he said flatly. "The Aversa carpetbaggers are gone, along with their distasteful son, Don Gaspare."

Her ears deceive her. Annulled? Sent away? Had she guessed the truth? Did Burchard tell her uncle of their secret kiss? How could such an innocent encounter warrant such an extreme outcome?

"Why?" she bleated, her voice barely a whisper.

"Alliances have changed."

"Changed?"

"I am Pope now," he said as if the position were new to her. "My supporters throughout this most difficult campaign need to know my high esteem for them." He paused. "My appreciation."

Her eyes stared blankly back at him, not understanding the connection between his elevation as Pope and the lovely white doves and clanging church bells sure to be at her wedding feast, Don Gaspare at her side.

"I am also happy to say that, as Pope, you and your brothers will now be received as my legitimate children."

"I am confused, Uncle," she said, a numbness swelling in her chest.

"He is no longer your uncle. Instead, you shall address him as 'father,'" Burchard chimed in, unable to help himself.

Tears stung her eyes.

"You are unhappy to be acknowledged as my daughter?" her father asked. "I thought it would please you not to hide in the shadows anymore. Live as a family. Whole and united."

Still, she did not understand. Lucrezia and her brothers had never lived in the shadows. All his illegitimate children, Cesare, Juan, even little Gioffre, and their other half-siblings knew Rodrigo Borgia was their father, no matter what they called the man before he became Pope Alexander. Most everyone in religious life had bastards wandering around. Did he think calling him 'father' now would soothe her? Make her forget the man he had sent away?

She jutted her chin at them. "What makes me unhappy is not marrying Don Gaspare Aversa. It brings me great sorrow." She paused and then added for emphasis, "I love him."

Burchard and her father burst into laughter. They snorted and choked, unable to contain themselves. Hot tears of humiliation pricked her eyes. She sat shamed, waiting for their amusement to cease. Her opinions, feelings, and desires all meant nothing to them.

Rodrigo cleared his throat and gained control. "Dear child," he exclaimed. "Two weeks ago, you called the boy a clumsy fool and accused him of ruining a silly dance! How did you go from despising him to being such a desperate romantic?"

Burchard raised an eyebrow, daring her to answer. Indeed, an unwavering stare told her that he had kept the escapade in the garden a secret and protected her from Rodrigo's wrath, perhaps protecting himself as well.

"I acted hastily. Behaved like a child," she stammered. "Giulia convinced me that marrying Don Gaspare would suit everyone's best interest, and he would make me happy," she continued, twisting the truth. "I fell in love."

"After two weeks?" her father questioned, dismissing her explanation. "If doing what is best for the Borgia family is important to you. If being a loving wife for the sake of our position is significant, then what I have yet to say will comfort you." He nodded at Burchard.

His secretary nodded back and read from a scrolled document. "You, Lucrezia Borgia, daughter of his holiness Pope Alexander VI, are to be betrothed to Giovanni Sforza, Lord of Pesaro."

A flush of rage seeped from her chest to her neck. How could she be promised to someone else so soon? Her dignity was of no consequence. "Who is this Giovanni Sforza?" she retorted.

"Calm yourself," Burchard scolded.

Her father raised a hand to quiet him. "The House of Sforza is reputable and needed. Cardinal Sforza is a devoted servant to both our family and God. He has assured me that his nephew Giovanni will be a good husband to you."

"I am a reward!" she gasped. A prize for Sforza loyalty! Cardinal Sforza's vote helped you win Saint Peter's seat. You think of me as a foolish girl, but I am not, and you will not use me in such a brutal manner." Giulia's words echoed in her mind: " He wants what is good for the Borgias. He wants what is good for him. The sooner you learn that, *the happier you will be.*"

"Be still!" Burchard seethed.

"I will not!"

Her father turned to Burchard. "Leave us."

Unaccustomed to being removed from controversy involving papal and Borgia affairs, the Pope's secretary hastily kissed his master's ring and left in a huff.

Her newly ordained father stood and helped himself to a handful of grapes on the sideboard. Sickened by the horrific news, Lucrezia approached the garden window and opened the shutters to let in what remained of the afternoon light and allow fresh air to cool her lungs.

"Lucrezia, why do you not appreciate my hard work? All the sacrifices and negotiations to become Pope and elevate my dear children from illegitimate commoners to apostolic royalty. Why are you so ungrateful? So selfish?"

He popped a plump, red grape into his mouth and chewed.

Her heart softened, but her anger lingered. "Ungrateful? Selfish? I agreed to marry a stranger, leave Rome, and live among his people. All because it was what you wished."

"It should not be such a hardship to do it again."

His words bore into her heart. How did he expect her to keep her self-respect? "You toss my affections like coins at a market!" she seethed.

The man she now called father whipped around, his white robes swirling. "Because you *are* coin! A Borgia coin! Do your part. We all must. Don't you see?" He waved his hand in disgust. "By satisfying the Sforzas, Cesare will rise to a Cardinal, Juan will become a papal general, and maybe even Prefect, and little Gioffre may gain a valuable marriage someday. The mother church is on uncertain ground, child. Pope Innocent turned a blind eye to the corruption that plagues Catholicism. Abbey and monastery coffers overflow with ducats skimmed from hard-working, overtaxed peasants who spend their coins on useless relics. That will end. I will see to it." He picked up the cheese knife and studied the blade. "I may be Pope Alexander VI, but the Borgias have many enemies, my daughter, rivals who would do anything to see me fail and cast us out. Never forget that."

She turned and searched the world outside her window. Rambling hills covered with dense forest and lush vineyards graced the landscape. The boy who had made her heart race was between the papal walls and those glorious hilltops, traveling back to Procida with its cobalt ocean - the same blue as her eyes.

"I understand."

***

"Dance with me," Cesare said, pulling her to her feet.

A festive song filled the reception hall from the vast music gallery above the crowded room. Platters of roasted game, boiled puddings, and braised vegetables were marched in from hectic kitchens, the first of many courses. Flaming torches lined the walls. Enormous candelabras held tapered candles, making the gold plates and cutlery shimmer in the light. The guests were a blur of bright colors and flashes of jewels. Loud talk mingled with high-pitched squeals and deep laughter. The air, thick with musk and perfume, burned Lucrezia's throat.

Several months prior, she was a commodity, a bartering tool, accused of being selfish by her father. Today, the merriment of her wedding feast encircled her as she sat and watched like a guest. Doves were released. Church bells rang. Even the banquet was more magnificent and decadent than Cousin Paolina's splendid show of wealth and power. Still, it did nothing to raise her spirits. She wore a white silk gown with inlaid pearls designed to look like delicate flowers. The flowing sleeves were sheer as gossamer and matched her long wedding veil. The weight of the dress made dancing difficult.

"He is old," she told her brother while he helped move her along. "He even smells old."

She had only danced once with her new husband, sixteen years her senior. The stench of stale clothes and sour breath was overwhelming, and she became dizzy.

Cesare laughed. "He is a widow and knows his way around a marital bed. Trust me, dear sister, expertise in that regard is good. So at least you have that to appreciate."

Lucrezia shuddered. The carefree life of maidenhood was gone. As a married woman now, duties awaited her, obligations not clearly defined but expected all the same. She longed for her brother's worldly experience, his sexual instinct, and his confidence.

Cesare's vast knowledge of intimacy was no secret. Although their father had advanced him from priest to bishop, it hardly impinged upon his many brothel trips. Instead, she spied him brazenly, sneaking whores into the palace and dismissing them the following day with a heavy purse of ducats. Was celibacy a fallacy? A made-up word? The longer she lived, the more it seemed men enjoyed two lives, the one they presented to the world and the private one that allowed whatever they fancied.

Cesare's powerful arms twirled her as if they were children again before drawing her close. "Be a good student in the bedchamber. Learn his tastes. Satisfy his desires. He will be good to you in return."

She squeezed him tight. "What if he is not?"

Cesare stopped abruptly and cupped her face in his hands, his chestnut eyes wide and intense. "Then I shall kill him," he said simply as if Giovanni's life held no consequence.

The words hung between them like a mist only they could see. Cesare threw back his head and laughed as he scooped a glass off a passing tray. "A toast! To my beloved sister and her new husband!"

Guests in earshot raised their glasses and shouted, "Salute!"

The celebration lasted late into the night. Surrounded by her new Sforza ladies-in-waiting, Lucrezia did not partake in the revelry and sat at the high table, waiting dully for the merriment to end. Giulia and Adriana were also there, sizing up the Sforza's women's delegation with their intricate Milanese headdresses and high, austere necklines. The women represented an array of young and old, carefully chosen from the Sforza court. The older women were there to instruct the younger girls as ladies-in-waiting, to help Lucrezia with her daily routine and obligations. Still, their common purpose was to spy and send messages back to Milan. Of that, Lucrezia was sure.

She searched the banquet for a sympathetic face, a hand to pat her own and be of comfort, but saw none. Cesare and Juan had both disappeared into the dark, seductive night, eager to get on with their whoring. Giovanni drank with his rowdy cousins and brothers, who whooped and hollered at bawdy jokes and lewd minstrel songs, which disgusted her even more.

Finally, her father rose from his dais and beckoned the wedding couple forward. Giovanni knelt beside her, the reek of tart wine on his breath. His damp hand fell into hers and gripped it tight.

"Rise for a final blessing," Burchard called out to the wedding guests, and everyone stood.

The Pope raised his arms, swaying a bit from too much wine. "Almighty God, bless Lucrezia and Giovanni. Bestow Your favor upon them. Keep them faithful to each other and secure in the vows they have taken today." His speech was slurred and thick. "Teach them humility and loyalty. Keep them mindful of their duties and obligations. Grant them long life and happiness. Amen."

"Amen," the wedding guests echoed.

The feasting continued as Lucrezia and Giovanni left the banquet hall and parted to prepare for their wedding night.

Her ladies, even the Sforza women, were kind and thorough. They helped her get ready, giving each other long, knowing glances as they did.

They bathed Lucrezia in rose water, loosening her waves of hair and brushing it with care. Adriana rubbed lavender oil into her skin. Servants brought her mulled wine. Lucrezia stepped into her nightgown, feeling relaxed and anxious all at once.

"Remember what I told you," Giulia whispered, tying the silk ribbons of her chemise. "And don't just lay there like a pretty rug."

"Will I get with child tonight?" Lucrezia asked, worried at the prospect of becoming pregnant.

"Probably not," Giulia answered. "Don't worry, there will be plenty of other chances," she added as if the lack of opportunity worried Lucrezia.

Lanterns brightened the halls and staircases as her entourage led the way to Giovanni's apartments. The procession was quiet, almost solemn, a far cry from the whoops and hollers and shattering glass coming from Giovanni's bedchamber. Adriana knocked on the door, and a sheepish-looking male servant answered it. He nodded at Adriana and disappeared briefly before opening the door wide. A stream of lewd, drunken men flowed from the room, stumbling and leaning on each other as they went.

Giovanni's older uncle approached Giulia, rubbing his groin. His face was sweaty and red. He leered at her pregnant stomach. "Too late. I see someone's shoved a cock in you already!"

Bianca, one of the new Sforza women and Giovanni's cousin rushed to his side and whispered in his ear.

Immediately, the man presented a low, sweeping bow to Giulia. "My sincerest apologies, madam." He wobbled to his feet and steadied himself on Bianca's shoulder.

Adriana motioned for two attending guards to escort the wedding partiers from the presence chamber and away from the ladies.

Were all wedding nights this boisterous and unpleasant, Lucrezia wondered. Once the room emptied, they proceeded into Giovanni's bedchamber. The bed was centered on one wall, facing a fireplace and sitting area. The ransacked room looked like a brawl had occurred. Discarded food covered the Persian rug. The partygoers had pulled down most of the silk bunting that had decorated the bedposts. Patches of red wine stained the coverlet on the bed. Chairs were upended. Only one of the incense thuribles remained lit.

Giovanni lay sprawled across the bed. His skin was pale and waxy. Lucrezia wondered if he was dead, silently praying for a timely deliverance.

As a blood relative, Bianca wasted no time pulling on Giovanni's legs. "Cousin!" she cried, but he remained motionless. Finally, she crept beside him and slapped his face hard. "Your bride awaits you! Rise, drunken fool!"

Giulia, Adriana, and the rest of the women scurried about, trying to make the room presentable. They righted chairs, lit incense, and hastily swept the floor. They pulled two seats by the fireplace closer together and set wine glasses on the table between them.

The women dragged Giovanni off the bed. He stumbled to his feet, supported by Bianca. Someone replaced the soiled coverlet with another. The fabric billowed above the mattress while the Sforza women on either side shook the clean cloth loose and let it drift across the bed.

Giulia guided Lucrezia to the fireplace and sat her in a chair. "Your hands are ice," she said, blowing warm breath into them. She handed her a wine glass. "Drink it. All of it."

"I am frightened," Lucrezia whispered, looking down at her pale blue slippers.

"All will be well," Giulia chided and lifted her chin. "One last thing. You may bleed."

"Bleed?"

"When he puts his cock inside you."

"Sweet Mother of Jesus, save me!"

"Shush," Giulia hissed. "Only the first time... usually."

Adriana appeared with Giovanni at her side. His eyes were sluggish, and his thick, unruly eyebrows weighed them down further. The velvet cloak worn at the banquet replaced a long nightshirt tied at the chest. His legs and feet were bare. Lucrezia stared into the fire as Adriana led him to the other chair and pushed him down. Servants tossed a log onto the fire's red embers.

Adriana clapped her hands loudly. "Everyone out!"

Giulia pecked Lucrezia's cheek with a quick kiss and followed the ladies as they exited, grabbing a pile of stained linen.

For the first time, Lucrezia was alone with Giovanni. They had circled each other from a distance over the past few months while the politics of their marriage were debated and completed. They had attended ball matches and palace hunts but were always in the company of their respective people.

She peered at her new husband. His face was fleshy. Deep forehead creases made him appear older than his thirty years. Although broad in the shoulders, he was relatively short and plump. He looked more like a street vendor than the Lord of Pesaro.

"Some wine, my lord?" Lucrezia offered, nervous and unsure of how to proceed.

"I am your husband. Call me by my Christian name," he replied, rubbing his forehead as if it pained him. "Yes, some wine."

She served him a full glass, which he swallowed in large gulps.

Lucrezia inhaled deeply. "Does something trouble you... Giovanni?" she asked, his name still foreign on her tongue.

His eyes scanned her face as if making an assessment and calculating his answer. "I am unhappy."

She stared at him in disbelief. How could he be unhappy? She was forced to marry and bed an older man who repulsed her. It should please him to be matched with someone so young and lively. Besides, they expected her to bear him many children and leave her family to join him in Pesaro. He may be drunk and foolish, but the thought of him being forlorn seemed ridiculous.

"If I may be so bold, may I ask why?"

He reached for the pitcher and emptied the remaining liquid into the tumbler. Silence hung between them. "Maddalena," he finally said.

"Maddalena?"

"My first wife. Our marriage only lasted a few short years before fever took her," he explained, his voice strained with grief.

Her mind raced, trying to decipher how to console her husband, a man she hardly knew, about his deceased first wife.

"We were an excellent match," he continued, not waiting for a response. Besides the alliance between our families, we were very much in love. She was a beauty, and she had a brilliant mind, as well."

"You seemed well enough at the banquet," Lucrezia said. The bawdy jokes and boisterous minstrel songs still rang in her ears. "Quite happy."

He lifted a thick eyebrow. "Life is a show, dear wife. Perhaps you are too immature to understand that yet. Would it please my father to watch me sulk in a corner? Ignore my family and friends? Would it please your father to see his daughter's new husband ignore his guests? Refuse the wine? Leave the venison untouched?"

"Of course not," she spat, annoyed that he thought of her as immature when he did not know her at all. "I do not care to be in your bedchamber any more than you want me here, or perhaps you knew that already?"

Giovanni finished his wine and tossed the tumbler aside. "Let's get on with it."

Lucrezia seized the empty pitcher. Panicked, she said, "I shall call for another vessel or some warmed mead."

"No."

"Some sugared fruit then."

"No." He stumbled to his feet. "Come to bed."

The fire had faded to a glow of yellow embers. Most of the candles had long burned out, leaving the room dark and chilled. When she made her way to bed, Giovanni was already there, waiting. His hefty frame rested in the center of the enormous mattress like a dark shadow sprawled on the coverlet, naked and still. She untied the ribbons of her chemise, one by one, feeling his eyes upon her. Finally, the

soft fabric slipped from her shoulders and onto the floor.
She stood naked before a man for the first time in her life.

"Come here," Giovanni murmured.

She peeled down the coverlet to climb inside, but he
stopped her.

"No. I want it on top."

She froze, not understanding. He reached for her
arm and, in one swift motion, flipped her on top of
him. Although not terribly fat, his body was soft like
a cushion. His hands reached for her breasts, squeezing
and kneading them like dough. His palms found her hips
and rhythmically moved them back and forth. Her eyes,
adjusting to the dark, saw his manhood between her legs
soft and flopped to one side. She remembered Giulia's
words about where his cock would go. She realized that,
in this state, Giovanni's would never penetrate her.

It did not stop him from trying. He flipped Lucrezia
onto her stomach and roughly thrust his groin at her
backside. His wilted cock slapped against her skin but
accomplished nothing. She squeezed her eyes shut and
imagined an island with a cobalt ocean and a boy who
made her body shiver. Finally, Giovanni shoved her aside
and collapsed on the bed, panting like a runaway horse.
A few moments later, he snored and mumbled, probably
dreaming of his lost Maddalena.

Lucrezia got herself dressed. She slipped under the bedsheets and rolled away from her impotent husband. So, this was what her father wanted. At least she did not bleed.

CHAPTER THREE

Lucrezia's mother, Vannozza dei Cattanei, owned a farm and winery outside Vatican City. Rodrigo had gifted it to her not long after taking Giulia as his new lover. One hundred acres of healthy orchards and robust vineyards provided a nice living for the woman who had birthed three of Rodrigo's children. His generosity towards her mother made Lucrezia hopeful that, in some small way, he still cared for the woman. Of course, it helped that the palace kitchen was an earnest patron, placing large orders of wine, meat, and produce every week. Her younger brother, Gioffre, still lived with Vannozza on the estate. It comforted Lucrezia that her mother still had the boy to keep her company.

Through household gossip, Lucrezia learned that
Vannozza had once been a courtesan serving the Roman
nobility as a young woman. Although the young and
beautiful Giulia had taken Vannozza's place in Rodrigo's
bed, her mother's rise to respected merchant made
Lucrezia proud, even if the Vatican court still viewed her
with disdain.

Dressed in a simple hooded riding cape of black velvet,
hair held in a trinzale adorned with silver beads, Lucrezia
slid from her mare's gilded saddle and handed the reins to
a nearby groom. The ride to her mother's villa had been
silent without the usual entourage of guards and servants.
It would displease her father if he knew she traveled alone,
but since her wedding a week ago, any company had been
a burden. Lucrezia cared not. She needed her mother.

Soft, pink rays of sunrise stroked the lush hillside, and
half-loaded wagons waited in the courtyard to be filled
with the farm's bounty. The villa was bustling with tasks
and responsibilities, even at such an early hour. Everyone's
duty was to work hard if any profit was to be made in
the daily market. Vannozza managed the vast farm with
passion and discipline, as she did her life. The presence of
the market wagons told Lucrezia her mother had not yet
left. She hurried to the outdoor kitchen, knowing that was
where Vannozza began her day.

Outdoor ovens and open cooking fires burned just
outside the kitchen's overhang, which covered long tables

meant for food and wine preparation. Barrels filled with olives, lentils, and barley lined the back wall of the house. Herbs tied with string hung from wooden beams on the thatched roof, drying in the early autumn air. The pungent smell of smoked meat and simmering grapes was familiar and comforting.

Lucrezia found her mother laying out carving knives. A bucket of coarse salt was ready on the table. For a middle-aged woman, Vannozza was a great beauty. Her thick, ginger hair was pulled back in a loose braid, and her statuesque frame and slim figure were both imposing and graceful. Her dark, olive-colored eyes narrowed as she inspected the array of cutlery.

"Mother?"

When Vannozza saw her only daughter, her eyes widened in disbelief, but after a few brief seconds, Lucrezia found herself embraced in her mother's strong arms.

"Daughter! What brings you here? I was not told of your visit. Does Rodrigo know?" She released Lucrezia and searched her daughter's face. "Something is wrong."

Her mother was always aware of her children's desires and needs, faults and weaknesses, fears and suspicions. Vannozza could see into their very core, which made lying nearly impossible.

Lucrezia's eyes filled with tears. "Father does not know I am here. I came immediately after morning Mass." She paused. "Giovanni, my husband, is also unaware," she stammered.

Vannozza's lips curled into a knowing smile. "I see." She walked back to the table. "Have you broken your fast?"

Lucrezia shook her head. "I have not."

"Sit," Vannozza said and nodded at a nearby stool. "But first, fetch yourself bread and wine."

Lucrezia helped herself to a plate of crusty bread and drink as her mother tied an apron around her waist and rolled her sleeves.

"Your father is well?" her mother asked lightly.

"Quite well," Lucrezia answered, aware that Vannozza had still not recovered from being cast aside. "The papacy suits him. He is respected but tells me of enemies who would see him fail. They resist his plan to restore the church."

Vannozza swung a skinned lamb onto the carving table with a heavy thud. "Fail? More like enemies who would revel in seeing him dead!" she spat. "All of us dead. Cardinals, bishops, noblemen, all conspiring to see us banished from Rome. Gone from this world, even. The market is full of whispers."

Lucrezia did not question her mother's words, afraid to further provoke the woman's hot Spanish temper.

"They tell me your wedding was beautiful," Vannozza said in a strained voice.

The statement pained Lucrezia's heart. Rodrigo had not invited her mother to the wedding or the banquet after the ceremony. As the newly elected Pope, Rodrigo had deemed it necessary not to draw attention to his former lover and wayward past. Giulia was his mistress now, but unlike Vannozza, Giulia was of noble blood. The distinction was as unfair as it was palpable.

Lucrezia stared at the cobbled stone floor. "Yes, Mother, it was."

"They also tell me Rodrigo's Italian whore is fat with child," Vannozza reached for a meat cleaver. Then, with several swift motions, she hammered the blade into the carcass, severing the lamb's legs from the body.

"That is true."

"His whore is your friend now? This Giulia Farnese?"

Lucrezia winced. "Giulia Farnese counsels me, as does my governess Adriana Domingo," she replied with diplomatic care.

Vannozza wielded the blade again, and the lamb's head rolled off the blood-soaked table. A mangy dog curled in the corner sprang to its feet and dragged the head away by the ear. Vannozza hissed at the animal, hastening its exit.

"Yet when you are troubled, you come to me? These women you call counselors cannot be all that helpful," Vannozza replied, savoring a mother's small victory.

Lucrezia shifted in her seat. "They do not know my situation."

Her mother scooped a handful of salt from the bucket and massaged it into the meat. "What is this situation?"

"My husband pines for his dead wife," Lucrezia said. "Her memory is a specter in our bedchamber. As a result, our marriage is not consummated."

Vannozza's face hardened. "You think that is his fault?"

Lucrezia's eyes widened. How could a limp, inadequate cock be her burden? "I do."

"Well, it is not. You are the wife now. You must make him forget his dead one."

It had been a week since Lucrezia's disastrous wedding night. Giovanni had visited her chamber every night since then but to no avail. Lovemaking had become a futile act of exhaustive rutting, and she reported the failure to Giulia every morning.

"I am expected to compete with a spirit?" Lucrezia answered, incredulous.

Vannozza's dark eyes narrowed. "Turn his yearning for his dead spouse into reality. Love him the way she did. Soon, his love for her will become his love for you." Vannozza held up a carving knife. "Think of a blacksmith and his metal. Your husband's dead wife is iron, but you are steel wrought from the fire after the iron's impurities melt away. Better and stronger."

"I don't love Giovanni. I will never love Giovanni. He is old and fat."

Vannozza laughed heartily. "It is not about love. It is never about love or even attraction." She pointed a salty finger at Lucrezia. "Remember that."

"Did you not love Father?"

Her mother stopped as if someone had turned the cleaver on her. Lucrezia froze, too, afraid she had gone too far.

"They will require an heir, your father, and that beastly Sforza family," Vannozza answered, ignoring the question. Her hands rubbed the meat with renewed vigor. "The trick is to make the process as painless as possible. But, first, you must take control, and that can only happen if you let the man think he holds the power." Vannozza laid out a burlap blanket and wrapped the salted lamb.

Lucrezia drank the rest of her wine. It was getting late, and someone would notice her absence at the palace if she did not leave soon. Vannozza heaved the prepared meat into a wheelbarrow, ready to load it into one of the waiting wagons. Her mother whistled through her thumb and finger, and a servant appeared and wheeled the carcass away.

"What does Rodrigo's whore advise you about your marital duty?" Vannozza asked in a casual tone.

"Giulia tells me not to lie in bed like a pretty rug," she answered cautiously.

A smirk crossed her mother's lips. "Then don't."

***

Lucrezia had lain with Giovanni long enough to know his
sexual tastes, his intimate desires. He liked to talk and often
mumbled to himself in a drunken stupor as he squirmed
on top, trying to mount her. Tonight, as with all the other
nights, Giovanni staggered through her door dressed only
in a nightshirt. Lucrezia was already in bed, propped up
on a pillow, when he made his stumbling entrance. Flames
from the fireplace warmed the chamber, and the air was
heavily smoked with incense.

Lucrezia had turned away the plain white chemise when
Bianca presented it to her, opting for a ruffled-topped
nightdress easily maneuvered down the shoulders.
Giovanni grunted a greeting and poured himself some
wine. He paused when Lucrezia pulled down the coverlet
to let him into bed, almost as an invitation, something she
had not done before.

"How are you this evening, my husband?" she asked,
attempting small talk.

Giovanni took a long draught from the goblet and did
not answer.

"Adriana tells me you hunted boar this afternoon. I pray
you were careful. The horrid beast gouged Juan in the

leg once. He still carries a terrible scar as an unfortunate reminder."

Giovanni grunted again and climbed into bed. "One less boar is roaming the woods to threaten your precious brother," he answered, unimpressed by the story.

"You are an excellent huntsman. Your cousin, Bianca, revels in telling me stories of your prowess with the bow and arrow."

He placed the glass on the bedside table and looked curiously at her. "You are full of talk this evening."

She wound a long curl around her finger. "I am only interested in your day, dear husband."

He watched with interest as she turned towards him. She posed on the pillow as if sitting for a portrait, ensuring the ruffled sleeve slipped from her shoulder.

"Shall I show you where Juan carries his scar?" Lucrezia whispered and reached under the coverlet. Her hand traveled down Giovanni's chest, pausing near his groin.

Giovanni took a deep breath, his chest rising and falling faster than before, as he nodded his answer.

Lucrezia's hand leisurely continued a bit more, then stopped again. "You are sure?"

He nodded again, unable to find his voice.

She tried not to grimace or even breathe as her palm rested on his soft organ, silently willing it to become firm. She left her hand there. Finally, Giovanni swatted it away, threw off the bed covers, and hastily began to dress.

"It is useless!" he spat.

"You are leaving?" she asked, trying not to sound panicked.

He yanked down his nightshirt. "What does it look like?"

Lucrezia's mind raced. Tales of Giovanni's impotent drunkenness would no longer satisfy Giulia, who was desperate to give Rodrigo good news. The marriage contract had to be made final through consummation. The situation must be resolved, as distasteful as that may be. She was the daughter of Vannozza dei Cattanei, a descendant of strong and determined women. She would make her mother proud, even if it meant fornicating with this impotent, grief-stricken idiot.

"Wait!" Lucrezia blurted into the stagnant air. "Tell me about her."

Giovanni abruptly stopped. "Who?"

"Maddalena."

He stood still, planted to the floor as if the name conjured a powerful spell. "Why?" he finally whispered.

"She was your one true love. Your happiness. I want to know this woman who, even in death, keeps my husband's heart captive."

Perhaps it was the offer to reminisce, or maybe it was her bare shoulder that somehow breathed life into his old cock. Giovanni slowly walked back to the bed.

"Come, my husband," Lucrezia purred, hand outstretched.

Entranced, Giovanni accepted her gesture and returned, the bed ropes creaking under his weight.

Without hesitation, she straddled him, ensuring that, this time, he would not get away. Her fingers lightly raked his face, closing his eyes as she pulled down her nightdress, exposing her bosom.

"Keep them shut," she said, mustering a commanding edge.

"As you say," Giovanni replied faintly.

Lucrezia placed his cold, rough hands on her breasts. "Your Maddalena, was she soft?" Lucrezia asked.

His fingertips squeezed her nipples. "Yes."

She bit her lower lip and reached down to stroke his cock. Immediately, the member grew long and hard. "Did she touch you like this? Your Maddalena? The lover that haunts you?"

His breath quickened. "Yes."

Lucrezia wasted no time. She shoved his manhood inside her, and after a few painful thrusts and a loud gasp from Giovanni, it was finished. She pulled herself from him and rolled over. Giovanni did not utter a word, not even a wish good night. Then, after a few minutes, snoring rattled the bedchamber. She jerked the thick coverlet over her naked shoulder, buried her face in the silk pillow, and sobbed. The consummation was complete. She had fulfilled the marriage contract, the obligation demanded by her father. Her fate was sealed. Her duty had begun.

Chapter Four

Late autumn surrounded the morning onlookers with a cloak of brisk air. The gathering of courtly ladies and men gasped and clapped, thoroughly engaged in the morning gameplay. Cesare and his opponent grasped their sword's iron hilts with genuine intent. They swung the long, gleaming weapons with brute force. Blades clinked and scraped as they wielded metal upon metal. The crowd whispered to each other behind gloved hands, wholly seduced by the Vatican's newest Borgia Cardinal.

"This Borgia knows how to handle a sword," Lucrezia heard a heavily mustached man murmur to the woman beside him.

"I am sure it is not the only thing he can handle," she replied with a wry smile.

Although the display of combat training was mostly sport for Cesare and his soldier comrade, an unsettledness had recently wafted throughout the Vatican court like a dangerous incense. France had suddenly laid claim to Naples after the death of Ferdinand I, and rumors told of French boots already marching across the Alps.

Cesare's talented swordsmanship entranced Lucrezia, perched on her metal garden seat. She marveled as he dodged and lunged at his opponent, quick and light on his feet, as he performed the deadly dance of combat. Her brother appeared carved from cold granite with his angular jaw and flourish of tawny shoulder-length hair. Sword in hand, his presence was calm and fearless. As a Cardinal, Cesare was quite the opposite. He was fiery and uncontrollable, like the wildfires that spread across the autumn fields. He was a warrior Cardinal, keen to root out those who wished to do the Borgias harm, and many did.

Cesare suddenly lunged to the left, and his leather boot caught his opponent behind the knee. The man tripped and landed on his back with a thud. "You are good, Alfre," Cesare said, the point of his sword imprinting a dimple in the man's neck, "but I am better."

"You win," Alfre conceded, careful not to move his head.

Cesare pressed perhaps a second longer than necessary but relented as Alfre exhaled a rush of thankful air. That was Cesare's way. Forever challenging boundaries, relentless in his conquests. The world was his to possess, twist, and control, like his many whores. He was good at everything, lover, brother, son, protector, all the attributes that made up a Borgia, everything except the Cardinal robe that draped his broad shoulders. The one thing his father commanded him to do, he despised. The weight of the red robe was a curse.

But her father's plan had been put forward and had to be honored. Cesare was to embrace the religious life, while Juan studied military maneuvers to become the Vatican Prefect General. Besides her father, the only one satisfied with the Borgia plan was Juan, who thought himself already a great general, even though he had only been schooled in the art of war.

"And, again, I let you live," Cesare teased and sheathed his sword, helping Alfre to his feet. "Worry not, friend. I will still buy the mead tonight," Cesare said with a wink.

Alfre grinned and rubbed his neck. The crowd dispersed, and Lucrezia handed Cesare his Cardinal's robe. Brother and sister strolled along the garden path back to the papal palace. Moments with Cesare had become elusive since his elevation to Cardinal. His new position had caused an uproar within the College of Cardinals, along with the other ten Borgia relatives recently ordained. However, her father excelled at Vatican law. He had the finest Catholic lawyers ready to serve him. Finding Canon

Law that worked in his favor was easy, and he wasted no time surrounding himself with holy familial loyalists.

"Your skill is impressive, dear Brother," Lucrezia said, entwining her arm with his.

"My skill is wasted."

"You see yourself as a great warrior but not a great Cardinal?" She gave his arm a gentle squeeze. "Father says the mantle of God on your shoulders protects us from inside these Vatican walls, while Juan's military expertise protects us and all the Papal states from afar."

Cesare's arm tightened. "What has Juan ever done besides drinking himself into a stupor? Who has he ever defeated or defended?" he replied. "Juan does not have the brains or the bollocks to save a songbird!"

Lucrezia found her brothers' rivalry tedious and their quarrels childish. Neither was ever satisfied with the position and power granted to them. She envied their freedom to have careers, be significant, and handle important matters, if only from the confines of their father's control. Unfortunately, she was not as fortunate.

"Juan will be tested when he confronts the French at Naples, will he not?" she asked earnestly.

Cesare stopped short. His eyes were dark and severe. "Dear Sister, how little you understand the urgency of Rome's predicament." He unsheathed his sword and drew a long line in the gravel between them. He sketched three circles, one at the top of the line, another in the middle, and the last one at the bottom. "This is France," he said, pointing at the top circle. "This is Naples." He tapped the bottom ring. "And this," he said, drawing an X through the center circle, "is Rome."

Lucrezia's mouth fell open. "The French must march through Vatican City to reach Naples? Is there no other way?"

Cesare shook his head. "It is the shortest route, but Father will never allow entrance since King Charles refuses to ask Papal permission."

"Why?"

"Many reasons. Charles has a powerful army and fearsome cannons and does not like being told what he can and cannot have."

"Just because he is King?" Lucrezia asked, incredulous.

Cesare shook his head. "Twice Charles was promised Naples. Once by Pope Innocent to punish King Ferdinand after he refused to pay feudal dues, but the disagreement was settled, and Pope Innocent withdrew the offer. Father encouraged Charles to take Naples during his papal campaign because he needed French support." Cesare paused and flicked a fly from Lucrezia's sleeve.

"But alliances changed. Father withdrew the offer again. Conquering Naples is now a battle of honor for Charles. Nothing will stop him."

"Surely our army is powerful, and our cannons just as fearsome!"

"French cannons are different. They fire chained balls that cut a line of soldiers like a sword through grapes. Bodies are severed, and limbs are lost. The tactic leaves behind a bloody, godless mess. France abides by no rules regarding warfare, nor should they," he added. "French soldiers are vicious and ruthless, while the Papal Army holds to the rule of mercy. It is our downfall. Our enemy will march on Rome while our dear brother, Juan, labors over stratagems to defeat them based on mere books and maps."

"War is inevitable because of the pride of both Father and King Charles," Lucrezia said, her stomach churning at the prospect.

"Yes, and Juan is charged with defending Vatican City." Cesare erased the ill-fated line with a kick of his boot.

Lucrezia slipped her hand back into the crook of his elbow as they continued their walk. "We shall surely be victorious. The French soldiers will see Juan and the papal army as a formidable enemy," she said.

Cesare remained silent.

"What about our allies?" she pressed.

"We wait to hear from the Orsini, Colonna, and Silvetti families. We wait for your husband's family, as well." Cesare's lip curled. "Has Giovanni spoken of this to you?"

"He does not speak to me about such matters," she lied.

Since his success in the bedchamber many months ago, Giovanni talked to her about everything. Married

for almost a year with no actual position except as
her husband, Giovanni passed the time training courier
pigeons and imparting his wisdom in everything. She only
half listened to anything her husband said. He was vaguely
amusing. Other times, Lucrezia swore she would go mad
with his constant jabbering. He was like a sentinel at
her side, lonely and alone, except for her, his pretend
Maddalena.

Lucrezia strained to examine the distant ramparts
surrounding the city. The thick walls felt less safe and more
vulnerable as she imagined chained cannonballs ripping
the stones apart, dissolving them to dust. Perhaps Cesare
was right about Juan and his lack of military prowess.

"What is your role in this war?" she asked, hoping for
brotherly assurance.

"I can recite military maneuvers and any Bible verse, but
my combat role is reduced to that of a counselor. I am to
offer Juan advice only."

"He is fortunate to have you at his side," she said,
although Juan never listened to anyone. "Tell me, as a man
of the cloth, if Father made you Papal General, would you
not choose to be merciful to our enemies?"

Cesare turned to her, his dark eyes deep and penetrating.
"I would not."

***

Lucrezia removed the cooled posset from between her legs. The thick cloth smeared with ground acacia leaves and honey was uncomfortably warm when first applied to her delicate organ. Nevertheless, she used the intimate medicinal after each encounter with Giovanni. Pietra had told her of the old practice used by her female relatives to ward off pregnancy. Lucrezia's first impulse had been to ask Giulia's advice, but why listen to a woman who had failed at handling the male seed and whose own baby daughter toddled around the Papal apartments?

Of course, she was supposed to carry Giovanni's child and bear his heir. Everyone expected it of her. But at barely sixteen years old, the thought of motherhood did not call to her—not yet.

Lucrezia pulled down her shift and summoned Pietra to help her put on her dress and clean up the remains of her remedy. After completing the tasks, her maid entered and opened the shutters to allow in the bright afternoon light. Then, wearing a rich green gown detailed in gold, Lucrezia plucked at the stiff folds of her skirt.

"The windows shall be shuttered soon, I fear," she said to Pietra. "There is a chill in the air."

Grapes had been picked, the olives gathered, the barley fields readied and planted, and the harvest season always conjured memories of her mother's villa. Still, lately, the biting air brought images of French cannons shattering the stone fortress of Vatican City. The thought planted by

Cesare that Giovanni's family withheld their aid haunted her.

"Is Giovanni with his birds?" Lucrezia asked.

"Yes, Countess, as always."

"I shall join him," she said. "Surprise him with wine and a food basket."

"He surely will be surprised," Pietra answered. A curious smile tugged at her lips.

Lucrezia frowned, the hint of sarcasm hitting its mark.

"Suddenly, you know my husband better than I do?" Lucrezia scolded.

Perhaps it appeared unusual to seek Giovanni since Lucrezia usually spent her days dodging him. Still, as her servant, Pietra was in no position to judge.

"The Count will be pleased to see his wife, of course," Pietra quickly said and stared at the tiled floor.

"Go to the kitchen. Get wine and dried fruit."

The maid curtsied, and the smile vanished. "Yes, Countess."

Lucrezia made her way alone to the roof of Giovanni's apartment, climbing the circular staircase carved into the massive wall. Now that she was married, Pietra's scrutiny had lessened. It seemed romantic encounters in secret places were no longer a priority for her father and Burchard. However, the idea appealed to her, even if Don Gaspare was a distant, youthful memory.

The tower attached to her husband's apartment was large and open to the air. In the center were two stools and a small table. Grain sacks were piled against the wall next to a tall rain barrel. Eight wooden cages stacked in a long row showcased several dozen plump, cooing pigeons.

Dressed in a simple tunic and cloak, Giovanni opened a cage and scattered feed amongst the feathered creatures.

"How often do they feed?" she asked.

Giovanni swung around, startled. "Lucrezia?"

She lowered her head. "Forgive me. I do not mean to disturb you."

"No," he quickly replied. "You are welcome."

Lucrezia crossed the stone floor and, with caution, peered inside a cage, careful to keep her nose clear of stabbing beaks.

"They feed twice daily," he said, a hint of hesitation in his voice.

The pigeons bobbed their heads and pecked the cage floor clean. Giovanni's hand moved skillfully as he reached inside to deliver the meal. His face was serene, and his voice soft as he cooed and clucked back to them. He moved to the next cage, but instead of scattering feed, he pulled out a plump pigeon and offered it to her.

Her head shook. "I couldn't."

"You can," Giovanni replied, nestling the bird in her arms.

The pigeon did not flutter or attempt to fly away as she feared but wiggled down against her warmth as if adjusting in a nest. Instinct drew her hand to the bird's downy feathers. "So soft," she said and smiled at her husband.

Giovanni smiled back. "Don't be fooled by their delicate nature. They are birds of war and can fly great distances. They are brave and strong, like a warrior, not frightened by the chaos of battle."

"How do you tell them apart?" she asked.

Giovanni raised an eyebrow. "Madam?"

"The males from the females? How do you know?"

He cleared his throat. "Their sex parts are difficult to identify."

Lucrezia smirked and stifled a giggle.

"Males have larger beaks and crops," Giovanni stammered. "Males stand taller, more erect."

Her blue eyes stared into his, wide with merriment. Slowly, his down-turned mouth melted into a grin, and they both laughed.

"Best take it back now," she said and handed the bird to him.

As Giovanni returned the bird to its cage, Pietra appeared with a basket and a vessel of wine. She opened the lid and placed a bowl of figs, cheese, and grapes on the table, along with two glasses.

"What is this?" Giovanni asked.

"Food," Lucrezia answered. "Come. Sit."

Giovanni locked the last cage and joined her at the table. Pietra poured the wine.

"You are here to tell me something, not just admire my birds," he said, taking a hearty draught of wine.

The time for games had ended. "You are dismissed," she told Pietra, waiting until she heard the girl's footsteps descend the stairs.

Lucrezia knew nothing of war but had a heightened awareness after her conversation with Cesare, noticing Juan and his military advisors meeting with her father daily. The tenor in the palace on the subject swelled like a wave, and the undercurrent of chatter was always underfoot. She felt compelled to do her part, as small as it was.

"What role will your pigeons of combat play in the war between Rome and France?" she asked, her voice direct and serious. "Will they fly for King Charles or my father, Pope Alexander? The French approach Florence. Their arrival at Vatican City is certain."

Giovanni's eyes narrowed. "No one has asked my birds to fly for anyone," he said, swirling the wine in his glass.

"What of your family, then?" she countered. "Who will they fly for?"

"Your sudden interest in warfare is intriguing, dear Lucrezia. How has this come to pass?"

"French cannonballs that can destroy Vatican walls have come to pass."

She took the knife and carved off a chunk of cheese. "The information drew my attention very much. Does it not pique your interest, or are you as carefree as your pigeons?"

"The French are coming," he acknowledged, brushing his sleeves of stray grain. "As for my family? I have heard nothing."

"They do not advise you?"

"I am a bastard. My family cares little about my existence. Although I am Lord of Presaro, I have no real power. Since my father's death, I am moved like a pawn at the whim of relatives." He paused. "Like you."

His eyes, with their wayward brows, held a potent sorrow that passed between them, raw and unspoken, as if they acknowledged each other's nakedness for the first time.

"None of this is of our choosing," she agreed.

His eyes clouded. "My sister Lidia was fifteen when my relatives married her to a Florence earl. Lidia was a golden girl, light and joyful, full of carefree wonder. She played the harp and lulled me to sleep while my mother bedded other men, not my father. Lidia married a rich and powerful earl." He took another long draught of wine. "Cruel, too, but he owned much land and gave the Sforzas an important alliance. I was only ten, but I remember the tears that replaced the light in Lidia's blue eyes when told of her future."

Lucrezia sat frozen on the stool. What was the purpose of this story?

"After Lidia left Milan, I never saw her again. She died in childbirth the following year."

"I am sorry," Lucrezia said quietly.

"Milan and Florence are no longer allies," he continued. "They no longer speak." Giovanni held out his hands. "What was it all for?"

Lucrezia opened her mouth, but no words followed. The story tugged at her heart, but why Giovanni would share such pain remained a mystery.

The clouds in his eyes cleared when they finally met hers. "You were a child bride when you came to me. You are a woman now, a child no longer."

"That is true." Her back stiffened.

"And I wish I had been a gentler groom to you, kinder, with a better understanding of your delicate situation."

She drew a deep breath. Giovanni's words were unexpected. That he acknowledged his brutish ways brought a strange peace. The impulse to rebuke him lessened. "Perhaps since we are more alike than we are different in the eyes of our people," she paused, "we can be friends."

Giovanni put down his glass, struck by the notion. "Although we may be mere pawns and placeholders, I would like to be your friend."

"When my dowry is paid in full, you will take me back to your country. A peaceful life with you will comfort me when I am far from Rome."

Giovanni's gaze shifted into a quizzical expression, a puzzled look that made her uneasy. "We are not leaving Rome. You did not know?"

Staying in Rome with her family and the only life she knew should have pleased her. Still, the silent maneuvering regarding her life angered her greatly. No one disclosed this information to her. All these months, she waited for Giovanni to be summoned back to Pesaro and for her to accompany him as his new wife. Be a countess in a new land. She was a fool.

"It is written in our marriage decree," Giovanni said. "It is what your father demanded. In part to keep you under his control and protection and to ensure that the Sforza do his bidding. So, dear Lucrezia, do not worry so much about French cannons. Your father's allies will stand by your side as long as I am here."

CHAPTER FIVE

Lucrezia rushed to her father's library window, which overlooked St. Peter's Square, certain she had heard the boom of cannons. The vast piazza was barren, devoid of the chaotic crowds and worshippers. The scene was unnerving and only added to her anxiety.

"Daughter, it is not the French," her father said without looking up. "Not yet." Rodrigo sat at his desk, distracting himself with the latest abbey and monastery complaints.

But the French were near, close enough for Juan to surround Vatican City with the Papal guard. Dark smoke spiraled into the morning sky from army campfires, and even with the windows sealed, the vague scent of burning wood penetrated the air. Giulia rocked baby Laura in her cradle, crooning. Giovanni pretended to peruse a book while Cesare paced like a horse new to the bridle. Her father had called them all to his library to be safe. He reasoned it was easier with them in one place if the French infiltrated the fortress walls. Perhaps he thought book-filled walls would protect them when stones and mortar failed. Her father had even sent a contingent of soldiers to Vannozza's farm, which was frightening. The thought of her mother fighting French soldiers chilled her.

"I should have gone to her," Lucrezia said, her eyes still intent on the empty square.

"Gone to whom?" her father asked.

"Mother," she said as if the answer was obvious.

Her father grunted. "Fear not. When it comes to Vannozza, it is the French who should worry."

Giulia hummed louder and feigned not to hear the name of the Pope's former lover.

"Father, let me seek Juan," Cesare interrupted. "Something is amiss. The French should not be as close as I fear they are. I warned Juan to battle the French where their cannons could not reach our city walls. Why is he still here as the French make their approach?"

Her father shook his head vehemently. "We must trust Juan's judgment," Rodrigo replied, his forehead damp with sweat. "His decisions regarding warfare are solid, and his reasons are not for us to question. "

"Are they not?" Cesare challenged. "When the lives of so many depend on us?" He paused. "On you?"

Baby Laura whimpered in her cradle. Giulia picked up the baby to soothe her.

Cesare planted himself in front of a sprawling map of Italy on a table. "No matter what the outcome in Naples, the French must come back through Rome to return to France. Must they ravage us twice?"

Lucrezia turned from the window. "Can we not discuss terms with the French?"

"What do you know of negotiations!" Burchard scolded from his place behind her father like a raven on a perch.

"I know everyone has a price," she replied.

"Lucrezia is right, Father," Cesare said, "and we must find France's."

Rodrigo's fist slammed against the marble desktop. "We must trust your brother!" he bellowed at them all.

Laura balled her fists and wailed, but heavy footsteps and loud shouts drowned her cries that echoed from the hall behind the library doors. Lucrezia swayed and steadied herself against the windowsill. Was it too late? Had French soldiers overtaken the palace? Cesare drew his sword.

Palace sentinels swept open the carved wooden doors, and Juan's aide, Savio Vitelli, rushed into the room. On a bent knee, the soldier bowed his head, a silver helmet tucked under his arm.

"Rise and speak," her father commanded and outstretched his ringed finger.

Savio obliged the Pope with a light kiss on the cold metal. "Your Eminence, I come with news from outside the city walls."

"What does my son have to say?"

"No message. Our general says nothing. That is why I am here, out of concern for Rome," the soldier dared to answer. "Allies have not arrived, and the mood of the infantry has soured."

"Mood?" Burchard squawked. "What does His Holiness care about an army's mood?"

"Explain," Cesare said.

Savio stared at his muddied boots.

"Speak!" her father shouted.

"There is grumbling from the ranks. They think General Borgia reckless and ill-suited to lead," the man stammered, "particularly in the absence of allied support. He stays in the command tent while we wait for orders as the French move closer."

"Damn them to hell," Rodrigo shouted. "If they will not fight to defend Holy Mother Church, they will die." With a swoop of his arm, the books and papers on the desk scattered across the floor.

"It is not the cause they question, Father," Cesare said, redirecting Rodrigo back to the obvious. "It is the command."

"Which makes terms with King Charles even more urgent," Lucrezia said, her observation as real as Juan's failure.

Rodrigo rubbed the back of his neck and turned to Burchard. "Your thoughts?"

"A truce will come at great expense," his cold eyes falling on Lucrezia.

"How great?"

"We must appease the honor of King Charles. Repair the perceived insult."

"Christ Almighty! How much?" her father growled.

"Recent funds from dismantling Saint Anselmo's monastery could be offered. We have little recourse against our allies' transgression, but," he paused, his large eyes narrowed, "the balance of Lucrezia's dowry could also be given to Charles."

"I discourage that course of action," Giovanni intervened. "My family must have good reason for not being here."

Her brother answered through clenched teeth. "If God Himself struck down every stinking Sforza in Rome, it would not be reason enough for their betrayal!"

"Brother," Lucrezia touched Cesare's arm. "Do not blame Giovanni. He does not control Sforza decisions."

"Which is why his opinions mean nothing and should be kept to himself, Sister!"

She stepped between her brother and her husband, a buffer for Cesare's fiery anger in search of a target.

"We must know Juan's intentions," her father decided. "Go to him, Cesare. Find out his stratagem and, remember, do not overstep your role as advisor. This is no time for trivial rivalries. Decide whether negotiations would benefit us."

"As you wish, Father."

Cesare disappeared, eager to don his armor again, but not before tossing his Cardinal's robe at Giovanni, the heavy velvet landing across her husband's face. "Make yourself useful." He turned to Savio. "Stay. Protect them."

The soldier pounded his fist against his armored chest and bowed.

Lucrezia leveled a look at Giovanni. Why would his family dare not come to Rome's aid? She worried, too, about her remaining dowry. Her father withheld a good portion of the money to help fund and expand the papal army, telling Giovanni's father that the currency would be released once Lucrezia gave birth to a child. If the balance of the funds were to satisfy King Charles, what did the future of their marriage hold?

Her husband returned her stare with a frown, silently acknowledging that their fate was as tenuous as that of his crated birds.

"Are you in need of anything, Countess?" The papal guard, Savio, stood before her, his hand ready at the sword in case she needed rescuing that very moment. He looked about Cesare's age with a beard neatly clipped and iron black hair closely cropped. His angular jaw was set in a fashion that told her he was serious, as did his endlessly dark eyes firmly planted on hers.

"No," she answered, liking his masculine attentiveness. Although this soldier was a stranger, his presence brought comfort, especially in Cesare's absence.

"I wish to speak with Burchard alone," her father announced. "Giulia, take the child back to our apartment. The rest of you return to Giovanni's quarters. Wait for my word."

Lucrezia took one last look at the empty square and imagined Juan and Cesare in a heated debate over France and the fate of Vatican City. She prayed Juan would listen without obstinate hostility and hoped Cesare would offer sincere guidance and not advise with his usual condescension. It seemed like a futile prayer, but she offered it anyway, knowing that both brothers would have to answer to their father.

In Giovanni's apartment, Savio shuttered and locked the windows. Giovanni departed to check his pigeons in the tower.

"Where is he going?" Savio asked.

Lucrezia filled two wine glasses and handed him one. "My husband keeps courier pigeons on the roof. He is quite concerned with their well-being."

Savio accepted the drink. "Is your husband as concerned with your well-being?"

"He is kind to me," she said and settled into a settee near the fireplace.

"But would he die for you? Offer his body to perish in your place?"

Lucrezia reflected on her life with Giovanni. A romantic spark had not ignited, nor would it ever, but their friendship had blossomed. He took great pride in explaining how the tiny, scrolled message was inserted into a miniature tube attached to a pigeon's leg. Lucrezia blushed when he clapped and delighted in her lute playing and poetry recitation. They played board games and passed the time like two kept rabbits.

"I pray I never have to find out," she finally answered and meant it.

"You love him."

"He is my husband."

The soldier's impertinent questions were inappropriate, yet she did not rebuke him. She enjoyed the wordplay and appreciated such an alluring opponent.

"Husbands are not always loved," Savio answered.

"Neither are soldiers," she said, sipping her wine, "and, besides, husbands can still be dear to a wife's heart."

"As Giovanni is to yours?"

Lucrezia stared into her glass and did not answer. His question made her uncomfortable, so she asked her own question instead. "Tell me, why do the soldiers not follow my brother? He is Prefect General. Why do they undermine his command?"

The soldier took a generous swallow of palace wine. "Your brother puffs his chest with bravado. He barks orders demanding respect and deference, but when questioned about war maneuvers, your brother withdraws to his quarters, becomes reticent, even hostile."

Lucrezia circled the glass rim with her finger. "Why do you think that is so?"

"Some say he waits to be told what to do. That he lacks experience and expertise and cowers in his tent, unable to lead."

"What do you say?"

"I say he is afraid."

"You think my brother a coward?" she bristled. This soldier knew nothing of Borgia strength.

"No. Fear and cowardice are quite different. Fear is common in the life of a soldier. Fear makes you fight the enemy harder. It keeps you from dying on the field of battle. A coward runs from the enemy. A coward lacks bravery."

"Juan would never run," she said. The word "yet" hung back in her mouth.

"Your brother fears making the wrong decision. He waits for a solution to drift his way like a feather falling from the sky. In Cesare, his prayers are answered. Your Cardinal brother will show Juan the way."

"And Juan will hate him for it," she said. Instantly, she wished the words back. Savio probably already knew the rivalry between her brothers, but she was a Borgia, and offering intimate family details was beneath her.

Savio shrugged off the indiscretion. "That is the way with brothers."

Hours passed with no news. Servants brought platters of food and what little they ate, they did in silence. The gray sky turned shades darker as the day grew longer. Lucrezia moved braised rabbit around on her plate. Certainly, word should have arrived from Cesare by now? Perhaps the advisement had gone wrong and the meeting ended without resolution, no plan for negotiations. They wasted time while lit torches stood ready at cannon wicks aimed at Vatican City. Obstinacy fueled her brothers' lives. Ambition ruled their hearts. Working as one went against their very nature, but they were Borgias, the sign of the bull, and she hoped that today, the survival of the Borgia family would bring them together.

As day moved to night, Savio took upon the duty of lighting candles and poking the fire to keep the flames bright. He was jumpy, not accustomed to waiting, not like herself and Giovanni, whose lives lingered at the whim of others. After a few more hours even Savio loosened his chest plate and retired to a chair, the day's mood taking a toll.

Lucrezia battled to keep her eyes open. If the French raided the palace, she had to be alert and ready to flee. She tried to recall secret passages Burchard had shown her when she first arrived at the palace, but she had been a foolish child then, and such things held little importance. She was about to give in to exhaustion when a hard knock on the door jolted them from their stupor. Two guards flung open the doors, allowing Cesare entrance.

Lucrezia rushed to him. "Brother! I feared you would never return! Did you speak with Juan? Have you seen the French?"

Cesare's face was drawn and weary, but a winning glow hinted that perhaps all was not lost.

"Envoys traveled between Rome and the French encampment all day, dear Sister." He collapsed into a chair and accepted wine from Savio. "King Charles finally agreed to terms. His army will pass through Vatican City. His coffers loaded with Vatican gold."

"And the balance of my dowry promised to the Sfzoras?"

"Your remaining dowry will fill them as well."

Cesare raked his hand through his disheveled hair. "We will seal the agreement at a banquet celebration in two days. Everyone will attend."

Lucrezia planted her hands on her hips. She did not want to argue with Cesare at this late hour, but breathing the same air as King Charles was too much to bear. The man's cannons haunted her sleep, and his greed had stolen what was left of her dowry. "I will not share a meal with the fiend King Charles."

Cesare sighed. "You will. Father demands it. We will show a unified front. A strong, if not happy, family. The king must see our eagerness to comply."

"Without the rest of my dowry, what will become of my marriage?" she asked sharply.

"That is for Father to decide," Cesare answered, rising to take his leave. "At least, for now, Rome is saved."

***

Lucrezia stared at the man seated next to her father. King Charles was not the creature she imagined, at least not in appearance. His plain, narrow face and beaked nose were French by nature. Waves of auburn hair stopped at his shoulders, and his light brown eyes were hardly unkind. The king was fairly tall but quite thin, rather willowy. Imagining someone so slight in physique leading men to battle proved difficult. His golden armor encrusted with jewels and simple crown were the only clues to his royal position.

King Charles insisted the reconciliation banquet take place at his command tent about a mile from Vatican City. He meant for the Borgias to come to him, a show of humility and respect. Outside the enormous tent stood the cannons that had caused her nightmares, the long iron shafts and neatly stacked balls a reminder of French strength and brutality. Inside the tent, long tables had been arranged in a rectangular fashion. Despite being an encampment, servants offered fine French cuisine. Roasted pheasant with wild fennel and carrots, boar stewed in thick gravy, and a delicate pear and ginger pudding were only a few of the many offerings.

Dinner was a celebratory affair with France's top military leaders, who were still high from the win over the entrance into the Vatican. Her father ate with a renewed appetite for a man in the depths of defeat. Conversation with the king was cordial, and even Cesare spoke lightheartedly with the French generals and lieutenants. Juan's absence was hardly noticed. After her father threatened to drag him by the ear to the banquet, Juan disappeared. Not even in his favorite brothel was he found. Once or twice, Lucrezia felt the king's gaze upon her, but she lowered her eyes and concentrated on her pear pudding, not wishing to encourage direct dialogue.

After the servants cleared the banquet plates and poured more Bordeaux, the king stood and addressed Giovanni.

"With your permission, I would like for your wife, Lucrezia, to take in the air with me. Perhaps point out some of the natural landmarks that grace the hills of Rome."

Lucrezia shot Giovanni an urgent look that conveyed a stroll would not be welcome, but her husband blushed and sat taller in his chair, happy to be recognized and readily agreed. Lucrezia bit the inside of her cheek and swallowed the surge of anger, telling herself that giving in to the king's request was her Borgia duty and another way of sealing the peace Cesare had worked so hard to accomplish.

The afternoon air was pungent with smoke from hundreds of small campfires. Soldiers ate from pots hung from tripods over coals. Horses whinnied for attention. Lucrezia pulled her velvet cloak tighter and prayed for a rain shower to cut their walk short, but the bright blue sky held little promise. Alone with the man who held her future in his coffers, she waited to see what kind of tête-à-tête her French companion had planned. Their walk took them to a small clearing with small fig trees and wildflowers. A butterfly descended upon a brilliant red poppy.

"Your country is beautiful," Charles finally said, admiring the scenery.

He had been quiet for most of their walk, allowing her to lead and impart her knowledge of nature and horticulture, intentionally steering clear of politics.

His eyes moved from the bright flowers to her face, "but not as lovely as you."

"You say that because I am a countess," she replied, blushing.

"I say it because you are the most magnificent woman I have ever seen."

Lucrezia bristled. "What of Queen Anne, your wife? Would she agree?" she dared to ask.

"They crowned me king when I was twelve. My elder sister guided me until I was ready to rule. They betrothed me to Anne of Brittany with no say in the matter. Neither of us held much affection for each other, but we have always maintained great respect. Privately, we lead our own lives. Publicly, we run the Valais Monarchy flawlessly." His mouth widened in a broad grin. "So yes, Lucrezia, my wife would agree."

Her cheeks flushed with heat. "Would you have been king if the choice had been yours?" she asked, eager to change the subject.

"Of course!" he exclaimed. "Only a fool would scoff at the will of God!"

Lucrezia took a deep breath. "Is it God's will or pride that makes you desire Naples?" she asked, changing her mind regarding political talk. "Why would you want land so far removed from your country? Have you seen Naples? It is rather dull."

Charles looked surprised but answered. "Pride is a wave that swells and curls. It crests and topples over whatever is in the way, dear Lucrezia. God's will guides me, not pride."

"Rome is in your way," she challenged.

"Yet I choose not to topple it."

"You choose gold instead and lots of it."

"Would you rather I consider the alternative?"

"I would not," she replied, not wanting the conversation to turn dark.

"France controlled Naples long before Spain took it, yet the Papacy offers Naples as if the land never belonged to the French in the first place," he explained. "They dangle it like meat whenever the opportunity suits their mood."

"I know the history of Pope Innocent, his offer of Naples, and his withdrawal," she acknowledged. I understand my father's folly, too, in that regard."

"Then you realize why I must take it back, dull or not. It is my right."

"Perhaps it is your right," she replied, turning to face him, "but... is it right?"

The king watched as the yellow butterfly flew away. "Right or wrong, it will be done."

CHAPTER SIX

Peace with the French brought a sweet and easy sleep. Lucrezia's feigned headache to escape morning Mass allowed a few more peaceful moments in bed, alone and relaxed.

She rolled onto her back and contemplated the mural of Saint Anne spread across the vaulted ceiling. The kindly-faced saint sat with an open book, teaching a young Virgin Mary to read. Holy Mary's hands were folded reverently, but her preoccupied eyes gazed upwards at the naked cherubs hovering in the billowing clouds of blue and pink. Lucrezia smiled. The scene reminded her of her long hours with Sister Angelina droning on endlessly as she sat distracted and bored. It was a sin to think of the old nun that way, and she silently admonished herself before rolling back onto her stomach, vowing to think purer thoughts. Now that the French army had carried off the rest of her marriage dowry, her uncertain future troubled her. Yet, she was secure in the knowledge that Giovanni could never be sent away. They had stood before the eyes of God, before the people of Rome. Dividing what God had brought together was sacrilege. Her father had spoken the words.

Her bedchamber door creaked open, and Lucrezia lifted her head to advise Pietra that she was not ready to rise, but the girl's eyes were wide with worry.

"Countess, a male servant is here from your husband's apartments! He says you must come quick, as the matter is urgent!"

"Can it not wait?" Lucrezia groaned, stretching her arms out over the soft coverlet.

Pietra's hands twisted fretfully. "There is blood on the servant's tunic," she replied in an anxious whisper.

Lucrezia tore off the blanket and scrambled to her feet. She rushed from the bedchamber to Giovanni's quarters without waiting for Pietra or the manservant. Lucrezia had dined with her husband the night before. All had seemed well. He talked of expanding his pigeon flock, even offering their service to the papal guard. She told him it pleased her that his plans brought him great joy, and she reveled in seeing him so happy.

"Giovanni? Husband!" she cried. His receiving room and bedchamber were empty, and there was no sign of blood. "Giovanni! Where are you?"

She heard movement from the pigeon tower above and raced up the stone steps.

He sat cross-legged on the cobbled floor, Giovanni and his pigeons. All the birds were dead. Blood smeared the walls like a devilish fresco. Someone had hacked the wooden crates open. Feathers and pink innards lay in pools of crimson blood. Giovanni held pieces of his slashed birds in each hand as if they were a puzzle to piece back together.

His eyes stared at nothing, vacant yet filled with horror. Lucrezia lightly touched his shoulder. His body twitched as if touched by fire.

"This was Juan's doing," he said in a voice full of accusation. "Your brother, the great Borgia General. My male servant watched him leave while I was at Mass, his sword bloodied. He can't lead an army, but he can slay innocent pigeons like a murderous coward."

Tears stung her eyes. "I am sorry," she whispered, horrified by Juan's brutal act. "You are right. It was cowardly."

"You? Sorry? Did you murder my birds? Was it your hand on the sword's hilt?" he asked incredulously. "No. Of all the Borgia's, you alone are incapable of such cruelty."

"I am sorry my brother is a monster," she replied. "Why would he do this? Why would he do this to you? They were harmless birds."

"Because he wanted to hurt me! Punish me for my family's betrayal! For not coming to his side to defeat the French!"

She sunk beside him on the bloody floor, not caring about her white nightdress. "Father will punish Juan. I promise."

His mournful eyes took on a look of pity. "You have grown much since we first met, but sometimes your naivete is breathtaking." He swallowed hard. "No punishment will come of this. No reckoning. Cry to your father, the powerful Pope. See what good it does."

His words pained her but rang true. Running to her father was pointless. Rodrigo would never hand down justice for Giovanni and his slaughtered birds. Nevertheless, she would guarantee that Juan would be condemned for the evil deed.

Lucrezia gently pressed Giovanni's hands against her own, ignoring the gory mess. "The Pope may not care about his son's wickedness, but I care and will ensure the world knows it too."

Giovanni removed his hands from hers and turned away. "Go now. I wish to be alone."

***

Lucrezia's determined walk to her father's apartments was met with horrified stares and gaping mouths. Lucrezia wore her blood-stained nightdress like an angry beacon. The scene of the carnage she had just left seared forever in her mind.

A palace guard approached with trepidation. "Countess, you are bleeding!"

"I am not," she replied curtly, staring at her father's apartment door. "Open it!" she ordered the two guards flanking the entrance.

Their faces remained stoic and blank. Panic washed over her. Did her command mean nothing? Were her words so powerless? After an uncertain pause, the men in their polished breastplates and red-plumed helmets thumped their steel lances against the tiled floor. They swept open a path for Lucrezia and her rage.

The Pope's apartments differed from the other embedded apostolic quarters. An outer channel of rooms insulated the more personal chambers. Lucrezia breezed through the waiting hall, past the inner receiving room, and into the Pope's intimate quarters. Her bloody arrival provoked the same alarming response from the nuns sweeping the corridor leading to the Pope's bedchamber. Still, Lucrezia's steadfast resolve cleared the way, and the nuns lowered their heads and busied themselves with their brooms.

Giulia sat on the Pope's bed, bouncing Laura on her lap. The baby, dressed in a heavily embroidered silver gown, giggled with glee like a miniature princess. However, the rhythm of Giulia's game ceased when Lucrezia burst into the room.

"Where is my father?" she demanded.

"What has happened?" Giulia asked, her wide eyes locked on Lucrezia's stained nightdress. "Is that your blood?"

"It is not! Where is my father!" Lucrezia yelled again, not caring if she startled baby Laura.

"The roof gardens. Entertaining your brothers." Giulia briskly handed her daughter to a wet nurse and hurried to her feet. "Whatever has happened, tell me before you make the matter worse!"

Lucrezia cared little for the useless guidance the Pope's mistress wished to impart. Nothing would bring Giovanni's beloved birds back. No amount of enlightened wisdom would heal that wound. Anger shook her to the core, and the need for retaliation and justice consumed her. Ignoring Giulia's warning, Lucrezia turned and dashed up the garden stairs, her youthful strides climbing two steps at a time.

Giulia set out after her, encumbered by the weighted skirts of her beaded gown, but her determined gait soon caught up. She grabbed Lucrezia's arm. "Stop!" she seethed, her breath long and labored.

Lucrezia tore from Giulia's grip and entered the ivy-covered walls of the garden. Cesare, Juan, and her father sat breaking their morning fast around an iron table filled with platters of seasonal fruit, loaves of bread, and vessels of wine. They grinned at one another as if they had just shared a bawdy joke or off-colored story, the positive outcome with the French still fresh. Their smiles quickly vanished when Lucrezia stormed upon them, barefoot and still in her bedclothes. Her father's face was ashen at the blood smeared across his daughter's nightdress.

Giulia suddenly appeared beside her, winded and disheveled. "She is unharmed, Rodrigo," Giulia panted before her father could get the words out.

"What has happened, Daughter?" her father said, the color returning to his pallid cheeks.

All eyes fell on Lucrezia, waiting for a tale explaining the state of her undress and brazen disruption of their morning meal.

"Juan slaughtered my husband's birds," Lucrezia shrieked and pointed at her brother, sounding more like a wronged child than an outraged wife.

"Birds?" her father's eyes were incredulous as he sat back and interlaced his fingers on his lap.

Cesare reached for the wine vessel; his eyebrows lifted in amusement. "All this fuss over fowl? The way you barged in here, I thought perhaps the French changed their mind and had stormed the palace."

Her brothers exchanged roguish glances.

"The birds were harmless pigeons kept by my husband," Lucrezia replied indignantly.

Rodrigo turned to Juan. "What of these birds?"

Her brother waved a hand as if the subject held little importance. "Lucrezia's husband kept courier pigeons in his tower. Pigeons that can send messages to enemies and return with replies. Who knows what secrets this Sforza traitor sent to his family?"

"He is not a traitor!" Lucrezia shot back.

"He is a Sforza."

"Your brother is right, Daughter. Juan's utmost responsibility is protecting the Borgia family."

"He murdered innocent birds that were only pets! A joyful distraction for my husband from these horrid walls that confine him! How in God's name does that protect us?"

Her father's nostrils flared, and his fist pounded the hard metal table. "You dare blaspheme in my presence?"

Lucrezia lowered her head and, crossed herself in repentance and inhaled deeply. "Juan is a child who threw a tantrum, nothing more. He is no protector. He is no Borgia general," she said with more restraint. "He killed Giovanni's birds out of malice, nothing more."

"Careful, Sister," Juan cautioned with eyes like snake slits, "you tread on dangerous ground. Don't think your youth and foolhardiness are an excuse for disrespect."

"Respect? I do not respect you. I will never respect you."

Juan's mouth twisted into a smile. "Shall we tell her now, Father, of your decision?"

Lucrezia's stomach churned at the prospect that they had spent their morning meal deciding her future. "What decision? Tell me."

Rodrigo leaned back in the chair and crossed his arms. "Given the circumstances, your marriage cannot hold. We must dissolve it," her father said. "My daughter will not be attached to a family that behaves like disloyal traitors."

"You joined us before the eyes of God!" Lucrezia exclaimed.

"I did, and I will undo it through annulment, not divorce."

"On what grounds?"

"Impotence."

Juan swirled his wine glass as a wide grin spread across his face.

Lucrezia raised her chin. "Giovanni Sforza is not impotent. He a good man and dutiful husband," she corrected.

Rodrigo nodded at his mistress, and Giulia responded on cue. "The marriage bed was troubled from the beginning," Giulia stated. "For many weeks, they reached no consummation. I asked Lucrezia weekly, and she always told me no."

"And?" Rodrigo coached.

"Given dear Lucrezia's youth and inexperience, I believe she lied about finally consummating the marriage out of shame and embarrassment."

Lucrezia's legs weakened, and her heart pounded and thumped with anger and betrayal. Her delicate finger pointed at everyone before her. "You are the liars! Every one of you! You say and do anything Father commands. None of you have any honor or self-respect," she shouted.

Silence embraced the tangled vines and green ivy of the apostolic garden, except for the twitter of a sparrow that plucked the air like an invisible harp, leaving a wondering of what would happen next.

Cesare abruptly pushed his plate away, still full of apricots and dates. "Sister, are you content with your marriage with Giovanni? Does it bring joy? Are you not lonely? The man is sixteen years your senior. You even said it yourself on the day of your wedding. He is old."

"What my husband brings me and what he brings to our marriage is none of your business, Brother," Lucrezia replied steadily. At the same time, her mind raced with anticipation of what was to happen next.

An enormous chess game lay before her. The piece designated to her was of no surprise. The pawn was the least powerful of all the board pieces but, played wisely, held enough power to disrupt and create disorder, which was what she planned to do. A well-spring of trepidation filled her. An overwhelming sense that a deal was about to be contracted floated between them in the cool morning air. How she calculated the next move would determine her future and set the tone for the rest of her existence. Lucrezia imagined herself with Sister Angelina, learning the art of chess and strategy.

"Giovanni will never agree to such a ridiculous lie," she warned.

"You will convince him," Juan replied, his dark eyes slanted again like a serpent.

"How do you propose I do that, Brother?" she asked. It was no secret a wife was nothing more than a figurehead.

"You are a woman. The power you lack between your ears, you carry between your legs," Juan replied.

The crudeness of the remark was breathtaking, and she looked upon Juan as not her brother but a hollow man devoid of compassion and brotherly tenderness. "You propose my husband and I perform the very act you accuse him of foundering?"

"I recommend you do whatever is necessary to bring your impotent husband to our side," Juan replied, finishing his wine in one quick draught.

Cesare glowered at Juan in disgust. "Do not be vulgar with Lucrezia. I will not tolerate it. She is our sister!"

"She is a Borgia," Juan said as if the designation trumped all decorum and polite discourse.

"Enough!" Rodrigo growled, the tenor in his voice halting their callous volley of words. "If Giovanni refuses the annulment, canon law states he must prove his manhood in a public arena."

"What does that mean?" she asked, shifting her gaze from Rodrigo to her brothers, then back to her father.

"He must fornicate with you in front of an audience," Juan piped up before someone could delicately explain the matter.

Lucrezia gasped as a wave of nausea swelled from her stomach to her throat. "I'm going to be ill."

Giulia rushed to her side and guided her to an empty garden seat. "It will never come to that. Giovanni would be a fool to allow himself such humiliation," Giulia soothed, stroking her uncombed hair.

Lucrezia recoiled from her touch. "And what of me? Have any of you considered my dignity in the matter?"

"Giulia is right," Rodrigo replied gruffly. "Giovanni will agree and quietly slip away, and all this distastefulness will be behind us."

Juan studied the steel edge of a paring knife before stabbing an apple straight through the core. "He will if he knows what's good for him."

***

Three days after Giovanni's birds were slaughtered, Lucrezia still had not mustered the courage to discuss the dissolution of their marriage with him. That Rodrigo could devise such a plan unnerved her. Maneuvering his daughter's future had become unmistakably easy for her father, making her uneasy. Yet, no matter how Lucrezia's world continuously shifted, she became adept at changing with it out of sheer self-preservation.

The formal annulment decree waited on Burchard's organized desk for final approval, and they had ordained it her responsibility to tell her husband, and soon, before news of the annulment leaked to the Sforza's.

Lucrezia found Giovanni in the tower that once held his precious pigeons, the one place that had brought him solace, maybe even joy. Dutiful servants had scrubbed the floors and stone walls clean, not wanting their master to suffer the sight of such violence. Yet, despite their efforts, the gruesome memory remained. She approached and stood beside him as the autumn sun receded behind a silver cloud, his eyes intent on the horizon. Giovanni did not acknowledge her but did not move away when her hand gently covered his. For a few silent moments, there was peace, perhaps even hope that they could grow wings and soar into the bruised sky to seek their happiness.

Finally, he turned to her. "I know," he said.

"Know what?"

"I am to leave here in disgrace."

She drew her hand away in surprise and then silently scolded herself. But, of course, he did. Servants and spies were the same. She should have known that news would reach him in the three days she squandered, avoiding the issue.

"I am sorry," Lucrezia said softly, her heart overwhelmed with sorrow for the only person she could call her friend, knowing how awful the news must be.

Giovanni's face twisted with the emotions of anger and embarrassment. "I am not impotent."

"You must say that you are. It is the only way our union can end in annulment. It is the only way to appease my father. If you deny it, the situation may take a dark turn."

Giovanni smiled wryly. "Ah yes, your almighty father." He gazed at her. "So, you will say that I am impotent? You will swear to an untruth, as well?"

"I have no choice. I can do nothing. You know that."

He looked away. "I do, but I needed to hear you say it. I needed to hear you admit you would propagate the lie."

Anger swept through her. Was it a lie when the only way the man could fulfill his marital duty was to pretend he bedded his deceased Maddalena? She withheld the reality of their coupling, if only because Giovanni would bear the shame of her father's decision alone. He would be the one to travel back to his family and his country disgraced. It was difficult not to be sensitive to his situation.

"You must think I am the cruelest Borgia of them all," she said with a touch of defiance.

"They will marry you off again," he answered, ignoring the remark.

"Yes, when it serves their purpose."

Giovanni's face darkened with worry. "You are too young to spend the rest of your life as a pawn for your family to move as they please. Do not suffer the same tragic fate as my beautiful sister."

Lucrezia withheld further rancor, touched by his concern. The thought of her ever making her own decisions was hopeless. The probability of being free from the grip of Borgia ambition was impossible, yet hearing Giovanni's words aloud left her something to fill her dreams.

CHAPTER SEVEN

Pietra moved to each little sewing group in Lucrezia's formal parlor, offering afternoon wine and small cakes. If the Sforza women knew of the impending annulment, they hid it well, for they, too, were to be sent back to Milan with their carts and carriages in disgrace, just like Giovanni. So they kept their eyes down, intent on the task at hand, giving sideways glances to one another now and then.

Lucrezia tossed aside the half-finished embroidery. She brooded about how quickly her marriage would end with no opposition. No one lifted an eyebrow at the absurdity of it all. Of course, no marital love existed, but Giovanni's friendship provided security and freedom to move inside their lives without scrutiny. As long as societal appearances were upheld, they could enjoy a little independence. That security was to evaporate the instant each Cardinal raised their hand in agreement at the College of Cardinals that would assemble within the hour.

A week had passed since Lucrezia's talk with Giovanni over the unpleasant situation. Word traveled to Giovanni's family with no acknowledgment from the Sforza court. Her father planned to proceed without waiting for a response. He reveled in his strategy and the genius of ending the marriage without the scandal of divorce.

Giulia abruptly breezed into the parlor and crossed the tile floor with a dramatic flair. The Pope's lover swung her pleated skirts around and sat in a huff next to Lucrezia. She fanned herself without the benefit of a true fan. Instead, her hand waved the stagnant air like a windless flag.

"Your father tires me with all this talk of your annulment," she snarled.

Lucrezia picked up the embroidery again and busied herself with completing a cherry blossom on an empty tree. "How is this my fault?" she asked, unaware of the surrounding maneuvering.

"Betrayal, dowry, betrayal, dowry. That's all Rodrigo speaks of. I can hardly stand it. He walks about as if your annulment was the most significant happening in the world. Affection is lost to him. He pays no mind to Laura. He pays no mind to me!" she complained and crossed her arms against her ample chest.

"It does me no good to wish the situation to linger. It makes no sense to blame me for any of it," Lucrezia answered, secretly wishing the predicament remained indefinite.

Giulia repeatedly plucked at the pleats of her gown and smoothed them down, a nervous, futile effort. "No matter. This nonsense will end soon, and all will be as it was. The Cardinals are gathering with Rodrigo as we speak."

Bianca paused her needle in midair. The gold thread pulled taught. She glanced at Lucrezia. "With your permission, Countess, perhaps myself and the other Milanese ladies might retire to prepare for whatever circumstance awaits us?"

Giulia threw her head back and laughed. "Why? So that you can steal the silver candlesticks and gold hand mirrors? Hide our lace gloves and silk gowns in your coffers? Your fate is decided. You are heading straight back to Milan. All of you."

"You will remain in my apartments," Lucrezia told Bianca in case Giulia's accusation held some truth.

Bianca and the others bowed their heads and resumed their sewing in silence. As the unsanctioned head of the Milanese women, Bianca had been good to Lucrezia, insisting the new ladies of the court were respectful and dutiful in all things, but loyalties had changed once again. Giulia was right to remind Lucrezia that the fate of her ladies-in-waiting was not her concern. As always, the obligation was to the Borgia family. Bianca and the others would return to Milan with futures as tenuous as Lucrezia's, waiting for the next move, the next marriage, the next Countess to serve with the same duty and respect shown to her. A dizzying dance performed on life's stage.

Suddenly, the need to see it unfold overwhelmed her. The desire to witness the College of Cardinals consumed her like kindle erupting into flame. Why shouldn't she witness the vote that determined her future, her fate? But, of course, her father had already decided the outcome. Still, she needed to see how cavalier this assembly behaved regarding a life not their own.

"I wish to rest before afternoon maters," Lucrezia said abruptly, handing the unfinished linen to Pietra.

"I shall go too," Giulia said.

"You shall stay and keep our Sforza friends company," Lucrezia directed, already reassigning the stature of the Milanese women. "You shall remain, too," she told Pietra before the servant offered to attend. "Bring the ladies more wine."

"As you wish," Pietra answered with a curtsey.

Lucrezia exited the parlor, eager to leave the uncomfortable silence and get to her father's meeting hall before the vote. She swiftly passed her bedchamber door and ducked into the receiving room, careful not to be seen. The space was small, only meant for guests to sit and wait until escorted into more formal accommodations in the den or parlor. A fireplace, two high-backed chairs, and a small table offered a comfortable, yet simple, seating area and a large tapestry covering the opposite wall.

Carefully, Lucrezia lifted a burning candle from the mantle, mindful of the hot wax.

Without hesitation, Lucrezia approached the tapestry and pulled back the intricate fabric to reveal a narrow wooden door. A rush of frigid air blew into the room as she slipped through the opening and quietly closed the door behind her.

It was one of many secret passageways shown to her by Burchard after moving to the apostolic palace. At the time, it seemed a game to her, slinking through the dark corridors with the Pope's secretary, pretending to be chased by the Knights Templar. Now, the passages provided a chance to observe a crucial meeting of Cardinals who held all the power over her world. A small child no longer, it emboldened Lucrezia to watch it unfold.

"Remember what I show you, but tell no one. Someday, these passages may be your only means of escape," Burchard had warned so long ago to frighten her into understanding the significance of what he said.

Now, she strode cautiously, following the flicker of the yellow candle flame. The stone hallway followed an exterior wall and, at certain places, diverged into other

winding passages that led to other inner parts of the
palace. The stagnant air smelled of mold and rot. A mossy
film covered the stone walls and floor. Lucrezia hurried,
mindful of the damp, slippery path.

Besides the secret passages, small openings carved into
the walls allowed for spying. Lucrezia was still determining
all the locations, but the spy hole she needed now she knew
well. Cesare had pointed it out during one of the many
ceremonies held after her father's elevation.

"See," Cesare had whispered in her ear, pointing at the
portrait of St. Peter high above Rodrigo's throne-like chair
in the meeting hall. "The left eye of St. Peter is where
Father will spy on his flock of Cardinals and observe who
can and cannot be trusted."

The thought of secret peepholes to spy on friends and
enemies seemed exciting and mysterious. Now the search
for this little hole left her helpless and afraid of what she
may witness.

After a short time, Lucrezia took a sharp left, leaving
the central passage. The walls were wood instead of stone.
Her feet retraced the steps taken with Burchard. Suddenly,
she stopped, noticing a variation in the panels. She waved
the candle along the wall, wondering if she had gone too
far. Her fingers brushed the paneled wood until she finally
found the peephole cover. Relieved, Lucrezia carefully slid
a hinged bit of metal, no bigger than a ducat, to one side,
and through the tiny hole disguised as the eye of the first

Vicar of Christ, she saw the great College of Cardinals and the consistory about to begin.

From Lucrezia's vantage point, the sizeable rectangle-shaped room seemed enormous. She wondered if this was how God felt looking down from His heaven. The gilded walls held portraits of every saint. Some paintings showed scenes of how they lived, pious and good. Others depicted how they died, grotesque scenes of violence and torture. Since the portrait of St. Peter hung behind her father's ornate chair, looking down, all she could see was the top of her father's white skull cap. On either side of the room sat the red-cassocked Cardinals facing each other in two long rows, their heads covered with scarlet wool birettas. As always, Burchard stood to one side slightly behind the Pope, a tightly rolled parchment in his grip. The great hall was lively with the swarm of chatting Cardinals, lobbying their campaigns and strategies until Burchard finally called them all to order.

"His Holiness will begin with a prayer," Burchard announced loudly. The room quieted as the participants folded their hands and lowered their heads.

After a brief prayer invoking God to steer their decisions to the benefit and betterment of Rome and the Holy Mother Church, Rodrigo directed Burchard to read the items. The process of the meeting was formal. Each item proclaimed followed a discussion, sometimes a lengthy debate before a vote. The Cardinals argued their points and opinions as Rodrigo moved the debate along with the occasional nod to Burchard, who would abruptly call for a vote. The conference continued until Lucrezia noticed her father straighten in his chair and lean forward in earnest.

Burchard cleared his throat. "And finally," he began and then paused to demonstrate the importance of what was to come, "His Holiness Pope Alexander VI decrees that his daughter's marriage to Count Giovanni Sforza be annulled and dissolved on the grounds of impotence."

Even though the news was leaked beforehand, the hall echoed with a collective gasp. Rodrigo raised his hands to silence the upheaval.

"Furthermore," Burchard continued, "the marriage dowry funds paid to the Sforza family shall be returned to the Apostolic treasury immediately."

Cardinal Sforza, Giovanni's uncle, sprang to his feet. "This is absurd!" the red-faced man shouted, obviously the only one not privy to the information in advance. "What proof is there?" the Cardinal spat. He pointed at Rodrigo. "Your daughter has failed to conceive! That is hardly the fault of my nephew!"

Lucrezia shifted uncomfortably as the argument turned to her intimate affairs. No one knew the great lengths she had taken to consummate the marriage. If she had not become Giovanni's pretend Maddalena, her father's claim of impotence would have proven true. Tears pricked her eyes at the irony of it all.

Cardinal Sforza ranted on for what seemed like forever while Lucrezia watched from above. The Cardinal was not about to let the situation stand without a fight. His angry cheeks turned as scarlet as his robe, even threatening to investigate the Pope for simony until, finally, Rodrigo lifted his hands to quiet him.

"Tell me, Cardinal Sforza, have I not done well by you? Upon my elevation to Pope, I rewarded you handsomely. Did I not?" her father asked smoothly and nodded at Burchard, who referred to the parchment.

"Besides becoming Vice Chancellor to our Holy Mother Church, Cardinal Sforza gained the estate of Nepi, the convent of Calahorra, several canonries and was installed as Bishop of Eger," Burchard announced.

"Interesting," Rodrigo continued. "I believe the position of Bishop also comes with a salary?"

"Ten thousand ducats annually, Holy Father," Burchard answered solemnly.

"All this talk of simony and investigations leads me to believe that Cardinal Sforza won't have much time to perform the duties of such an important position. So perhaps instead of returning the portion of my daughter's dowry not presented to the French, the Cardinal will surrender the position and the income?"

The question was a veiled threat, and the color drained from the Cardinal's face as quickly as it rose a moment ago. He stood silently, not knowing how to answer.

"The question requires a response," Burchard said sharply.

Cardinal Sforza's shoulders slumped as he stared down at the floor. "I will notify my people. The Sforza's will return the dowry to the Apostolic treasury."

***

Lucrezia busied herself with choosing fabric and lace for the feast of Saint Isidore. Both commoners and royals alike enjoyed the harvest celebration. The outdoor carnival festivities highlighted the growing season's bounty and would be the last celebration before Christmas. Lucrezia's hand lightly touched the soft scarlet velvet, one of many laid out on her canopied bed. The heavy fabric would provide warmth, although, as always, dancing would be a hindrance. Little did she care. After the upheaval of her annulment over the past few days, merriment and dancing were not in her heart.

"Where is Giulia?" Lucrezia asked, curious about the girl's absence on a day that usually had her father's mistress pawing and primping.

"She is with the Milanese women," Adrianna replied, her words short and clipped.

"Fear not, Countess. They are watched closely," Pietra reassured Lucrezia of her former ladies-in-waiting.

"You will address your mistress as Princess," Adrianna chided, reminding the servant of Lucrezia's recently ratified annulment.

Lucrezia had been careful to leave the Milanese women alone as they packed and readied themselves for the journey back to their homeland. The royal apartment was quiet without them, even somber, as several nuns had taken their place until new ladies-in-waiting were assigned. Lucrezia missed them. Besides being attentive to her needs, the women provided companionship and a much needed female presence in a male-dominated routine.

She had not sought out Giovanni either. What was there to say? Should she apologize for her father sending him away disgraced? Giovanni had little to say to her anyway since Juan murdered his beloved pigeons. Perhaps he blamed her for merely being a Borgia as if the very name had somehow performed the vicious deed. Lucrezia felt shame as well.

At the festival today, she would be part of the palace entourage touring the many vendor booths and farm wagons laden with the season's bounty. Still, she would be unaccompanied, husbandless, and available once again on the marital market. She dreaded the eyes falling upon her and the whispers about her impotent former husband that would follow her around the carnival, casting a shadow of humiliation.

"Surely your mother will attend today," Adriana offered, trying to rouse a smile from her.

"My mother will be busy peddling her wine and meats," Lucrezia replied, holding back the quiver in her voice.

Vannozza had kept her opinion of her daughter's annulment secret, and Lucrezia was not eager to see her. Failure was not something her mother abided well, as witnessed by the woman's internal grudge against Giulia and her own failure to keep Rodrigo as a lover. Now, her daughter also couldn't keep a husband, or at least that was how Lucrezia felt, even though her father moved her around like a game piece. So today, it was time to wear not a brave face but an indifferent one, a Borgia face that showed no emotion to the machinations of the world. A visage that could withstand both whispers and stares. She owed herself at least that much.

***

St. Peter's Square was a rush of loud street vendors bartering their goods. Children scampered underfoot, eager for the game booths and sweet treats. Overloaded wagons, small stages, and makeshift stalls created paths

that congested the square's usual vast open space with
hordes of buyers and sellers. There were revelers, dancers,
and street musicians all swirling amidst the strong scent
of the perfumed upper class and the stench of unwashed
peasants.

The apostolic party entered the festival a united retinue.
But it took only a short time before Rodrigo and his
favored Cardinals were off sampling the wares of the
olive carts. At the same time, Cesare and Juan quickly
discovered the endless line of wine vendors. Giulia only
walked beside Lucrezia briefly before a puppet show
entranced her and baby Laura. Lucrezia continued alone,
but only partially. Woven throughout the Vatican royals,
and usually, only steps behind, were the Vatican guards.
The Borgias were always careful.

Lucrezia paused at a wagon overflowing with roses,
lilies, and gladioli. Picking up a long-stemmed pink rose,
she breathed deeply. The sweet floral scent was calming
among the chaotic revelry.

"The flower is beautiful," a familiar voice said over her
shoulder, "much like the hand that holds it."

She turned to see Savio Vitelli's handsome grin and
sea-blue eyes and silently admonished herself for staring.

The soldier held out a ducat to the owner of the flower
cart. The shriveled woman beamed at Lucrezia, stunned to
have a member of the Holy Family as a patron.

"Please, no," the woman said, waving the coin away.

Lucrezia took the ducat from Savio and gently folded it into the woman's calloused palm. "May God bless you and your beautiful flowers," she said, then continued with the rose in one hand and Savio by her side.

"Would you care for some company, Princess?" he asked.

The question was innocent enough, but Lucrezia was secretly pleased to see the handsome, charismatic soldier again. His striking smile and kind eyes were more than welcome, and she hoped he hadn't noticed the pink blush that rose to her cheeks.

"If you wish," Lucrezia answered, trying not to sound too eager.

The stares and whispers faded as they moved along the carts and booths. Savio walked confidently beside her, without swagger or arrogance, but as if they were just another twosome enjoying an afternoon of merriment. They came upon a group of musicians playing a merry tune and watched couples twirl to the lively beat. Lucrezia half hoped her handsome escort would invite her to dance and then sparked with anger when he did not. She scolded herself for entertaining such a silly thought. The idea of a soldier dancing with a royal was ludicrous. Yet, she could not help but imagine his powerful arms around her waist and his sturdy cheek against hers. She swallowed hard. It was easy to explain his presence as protection and nothing more. To think of him romantically was foolish. Yet there was a lightness about Savio that was attractive, a cavalier attitude that calmed her.

"I am unmarried now," she said suddenly, fixing her eyes on the dancers.

"Yes," he answered. "I am sorry for your trouble, Princess."

"There will be more trouble to come. Surely, another marriage awaits me, depending on the whim of my father."

The handsome warrior remained silent for a moment. "Forgive me, but your father does not seem to be a man of whimsy," he finally said.

"Perhaps not, but it is unnerving never to control your future, to live under a constant cloud of uncertainty."

"This you can be sure of. Your father loves you, and his decisions are made for the good of your family." Savio's eyes, dark and serious, narrowed. "My father sent me away for military training as a boy. I despised being told what to do and when and how to do it. But, as I grew, I learned that obedience and discipline strengthened the regiment, and the regiment was my new family. I needed them to be strong."

"So, I should be a better soldier," she answered, amused and touched by his story.

"I don't think you could be any more perfect than you are already."

The whirl of the carnival stopped at his words. Never had Lucrezia heard a more sincere compliment. Never had she been told that she was perfect just the way she was.

"You shall marry and have your own family someday?" she asked, her heart thumping hard against her chest.

Savio's head shook, and a grin spread across his face. "And leave a wife and family to fight wars that keep the beautiful Borgia Princess protected? No, I shall never marry."

"Then you shall take many lovers," Lucrezia replied, trying to maintain a smile.

"Many? No, just one," he told her as his gloved hand brushed her own.

The gesture was fleeting yet poignant. Lucrezia drew a sharp breath. Did she hear his words correctly? Surely not. Yet, she trembled at the thought. To have him dangle before her like a wanton dream made Lucrezia desire him all the more, but her palm struck his cheek before she could stop herself.

"You overstep your place, sir," she told him in a voice barely above a whisper.

The blow barely shook him. It hardly left a mark on his already ruddy, sun-kissed skin.

"Perhaps," Savio answered in a low, confident voice. "But I stand by my words." He turned and, whipping his soldier's cape around his broad shoulders, left as swiftly as he had appeared.

Suddenly, Lucrezia realized that the dancers had stopped dancing and the crowd had fallen silent with watchful eyes. She moved away from the stage, eager to lose the cold weight of their stares. She wanted to flee to her apartments, back to the safety of her walled rooms like one of Giovanni's little pigeons eager for the nest. But the little birds were dead, and she was alive with no place to find shelter. A young, striking man had just told her he desired her for no other reason than because he thought she was perfect, and what had she done? Slapped him away like a fly, something worthy of repulsion.

Lucrezia turned to make her way back to the palace, no longer caring for the carnival's whirring revelry, and almost walked into a figure that had sidled up quietly from behind.

"Make way!" Lucrezia sniped at the hooded woman in the long dark cape, her mood soured.

"Princess," a familiar voice whispered, "please save us."

Lucrezia looked closer at the down-turned face. "Bianca?"

The woman nodded.

"Why are you here? The Sforza caravan left hours ago. Have you run away? I cannot allow you back. Father would never permit it." Lucrezia kept her voice low and, linking their arms, led Bianca away from the stage. She proceeded in haste, weaving in and out of the revelers, fearful of drawing attention until Lucrezia found a quieter place near a vendor selling religious relics and vigil candles.

Lucrezia faced Bianca and held the girl's trembling hands. "What has happened?"

"Word has come that your marriage dowry will not be returned to the Vatican coffers as promised."

"Why? How?"

"A messenger arrived with news. The funds will stay in the greedy Sforza hands. They say it belongs to them, and the portion used to bribe the French was rightly theirs and stolen from them. That the annulment was coerced and our return is not welcome. They claim the marriage is still valid, and we must stay." Her hands shook uncontrollably. "Giovanni's family cares more about the coin than their kin. When your father learns of this, we fear his wrath. We fear he will send Juan to punish and murder us to answer the Sforza insult," Bianca gushed, her voice thick with dread. "Giovanni wishes to journey to Perugia, to the city of Castel del Piano, his uncle's home. He believes the man will give us sanctuary. We need your protection to get there."

"Why come to me? I am no soldier," Lucrezia answered, acutely aware that she had just slapped and sent away the one soldier who may have helped.

"Your brother, Cesare. He is a man of the cloth. He will listen to your plea."

The girl was wise to think of her brother. More than the reluctant religious cloth that draped Cesare's shoulders, the bond between brother and sister was strong. But his loyalty was to their father, the Pope, first and always. Any attempt to sway Cesare's allegiance would not be easy.

"Perhaps," Lucrezia answered, her voice low. "I will speak to him, but I make no guarantee. If he runs to the Pope with this news, I cannot stop him."

Several customers milled around the white candles and wooden crosses, close enough to hear. "Leave now," Lucrezia whispered. "If what you say is true, you are even less safe within the Vatican walls."

"Thank you, Princess." Bianca's eyes filled with grateful tears. "We are forever in your debt."

"Careful, I did not save you yet. Even if Cesare cares to listen, he may not choose to help."

Bianca squeezed her arm. "But you will try. You will do your best?" Her words were urgent.

"I will," Lucrezia replied, unsure that her intervention would make any difference.

Bianca turned away into the crowd, back to the convoy that faced destruction if Lucrezia did not act quickly.

Cesare was easy to find. The difficulty was dragging him from the bawdy drunkards surrounding the wine vendor's cart. Once full of rich wine, empty flagons littered the surrounding ground. Thunderous conversations flourished with boastful tales of valor and love conquests.

Lucrezia breathed deeply, letting the air swell in her chest as she approached her brother. "We must talk," she said.

Cesare frowned. "Go away, Sister. Find Giulia or your maidservant to keep you company. This is no place for a woman," he said, emboldened by drink.

Lucrezia steeled herself and reached for Cesare's arm, then drew back. To act like a little girl pulling at his sleeve was beneath her and would not strengthen her plight.

"I call upon you to fulfill a promise you made to me," she said loud enough to draw attention. "A solemn vow offered on my wedding day."

"A vow?" the man next to Cesare questioned, thumping her brother's back. His beard dripped with wine. "Was it to stop swilling and whoring? Because, friend, you broke those vows long ago!"

The men laughed loudly and drew nearer. Their interest peaked by the exchange and Lucrezia.

"I don't know what you speak," Cesare said, gritting his teeth. Can this not wait?"

"It cannot. Come with me. Perhaps the taste of honeyed water instead of overpriced wine will jolt your memory."

"Go away!" he retorted. "I am not your hound!"

Lucrezia pointed at her brother, aware of the spectacle she was creating. "You are no man of your word!"

Cesare's eyes flashed. "Mind your tone, Sister!"

"If he doesn't listen, Princess, I will keep Cesare's promise for him!" a voice shouted over the taunts and jests. "Especially if it involves his beautiful sister!" The group roared with laughter.

He slammed the wine vessel to the ground and grabbed Lucrezia's arm. "Let's go." His fingers dug into her forearm. Lucrezia bit her lip to keep from crying out. He pulled her away from the men and finally released her as they walked down the main path of the festival.

"You insult and embarrass me and expect a favor? Your ways of diplomacy are strange, Sister," Cesare said, not looking at her.

"My insult drew you away from the likes of men who would do you far worse."

"Ah, so it is you who did me a favor?" Cesare scoffed. "What is this about? State your business, Sister, and be plain. My head pains me from too much drink."

Lucrezia took his arm. "Not here," she said.

They left the festival telling no one. The earlier brilliant sun had become a fiery sunset. Royalty and commoners had gorged and feasted all day, and the revelry would last a good part of the night. The twosome hurried to the Basilica, where they would be alone except for monks and nuns. Silence filled the massive domed cathedral. The acrid scent of incense hung in the air. Under the vast dome, the baldachin, a great bronzed canopy supported by four thick pillars, covered the main altar, concealing the tomb of St.

Peter. They settled into one of the many alcoves devoted to the saints.

"You told me once that if my husband ever caused me harm, you would kill him," Lucrezia said, kneeling on a cushion at the statue of Saint Jude.

Cesare joined her. "At your wedding, I remember. Now your marriage is over, but do not worry, Sister, I will renew my vow when you marry again," he said wryly. "Is that what this is about? Are you afraid to marry again?"

"It is not," Lucrezia replied and told Cesare of her encounter with Bianca and the plight of the caravan. "You advised me to be a good student in Giovanni's bedchamber. Learn his tastes, his desires. I did that. Giovanni was not impotent. We consummated our marriage. We did our duty."

"Giovanni is gone. Impotent or not, he is what Father says he is."

Lucrezia stared up at Saint Jude's benevolent face. "Giovanni was a friend to me, and I to him. Would you save him? Would you save his life for me if it was in danger?"

"Perhaps he is not in danger at all. You know not what Father might do. The favor you ask may be a fool's errand."

"Father is accustomed to getting his way. What do you believe he will do when word comes that my dowry is lost? What does your heart tell you?"

Cesare massaged his forehead. "Father may punish Cardinal Sforza in retaliation, but the other Cardinals may become resentful. Since the Sforza family could not care less about Giovanni, the man would make a futile hostage. You might be right. Father may send Juan if anger overtakes him. He may kill your Giovanni as a lesson for other so-called allies who defy him." Cesare took a long pause before he continued. "I will go. I will take my most trusted men and see Giovanni safely to Perugia."

Lucrezia's face brightened. "I am forever in your debt," she said, grateful her brother would take her side.

Cesare rose and helped her to her feet. "You are kindhearted, Lucrezia. More than I could ever be. Careful, though, that your kindness is not mistaken for weakness."

Chapter Eight

Lucrezia lay across her bed, staring into the blaze of the hearth. The hour was unknown, but sleep escaped her deep into the night. Five days had passed since Cesare left to ensure safe passage for Giovanni and the Sforza caravan and long enough for Cesare to have delivered them to Giovanni's uncle in Perugia. No word had come, though. No message of success or failure. Her father was on a rampage over Cesare's absence and dismissed the explanation that his son was off whoring. Lucrezia vehemently denied knowing her brother's whereabouts. She wanted to tell her father that, as the bible proclaimed, she was not her brother's keeper, but it would have angered him further.

She mulled tossing another log into the fire or drinking some wine to help her sleep when she heard the bedchamber latch unbolt. As the door slowly opened, her throat tightened. Pietra would have knocked before entering. The only person who disregarded palace courtesy was Burchard, who came and went as he pleased, but certainly, it would not be the old crow at this late hour.

Lucrezia jolted up. "Who's there!" she called out.

The door stopped midway.

"One scream will bring the guards! Show yourself."

A familiar face peered from around the wooden door. "But, Princess, a guard is already here," Savio answered with a handsome grin.

The festival was the last place she had seen Savio. She relived their conversation that ended with a harsh slap over in her mind many times. Her behavior had been out of shock and, perhaps, fear. Although she had lain with a man, the thought that one might find her desirable was all at once exciting and frightening.

"What brings you at this late hour?" Lucrezia stammered.

"Cesare sent me." He closed the door behind him and strode across the room. Pulling off his riding gloves, he sat beside her on the bed. His silver breastplate held specks of wet mud. "Your Giovanni rests safely in Perugia. Your brother wanted you to know immediately."

"You went with Cesare?" Lucrezia said, knowing her brother would have only taken his most trusted men.

"I did," Savio replied.

"Why did he not come himself to tell me?"

"Forgive me, Princess, but your brother stopped at the brothel upon our return."

"Was there trouble on the road?" Lucrezia asked, ignoring her brother's indiscretion.

"No, but on the second night, your brother, Juan, and a band of his men stopped at our camp."

Lucrezia drew a deep breath. "What happened?"

Savio grinned. "Cesare convinced him to be on his way," he said wryly. Perhaps you were right to request an escort for Giovanni."

"How did Cesare manage without violence?" Lucrezia asked.

Savio drew closer. The sweat of horse and leather wafted from him. "The ways of brothers are between brothers," he answered, " although it may have involved harsh words and brotherly blows."

Not needing further details, Lucrezia gathered her nightclothes around her and reached for the wine vessel on the bed stand. "Thank you for the good news. May I offer you some wine before you go?"

Savio reached for her wrist. His eyes held a hunger she felt in his steady grip.

"What are you doing?" she asked, her voice barely above a whisper.

He drew her close. His words and the heat of his breath filled her ear. "Ask me to stop, and I will stop. Tell me to go, and I will go, but let's not play the games of children."

"I am not a child," she panted.

"That you are not." Savio lifted the silver breastplate over his head, placed it on the floor, and then turned back to her.

His face was close now, and the flames flickered in his dark eyes. He wrapped a hand around Lucrezia's loose curls as his arm encircled her waist, pulling her forward. At first, his lips lightly brushed hers, soft and timid, but when she failed to stop him, the kissing came with more urgency.

She felt his heat and a rush of wetness between her legs. Her hands held his face as her open mouth eagerly met his.

Skilled hands untied her silk nightdress, and, in one motion, the garment slid from her shoulders. For a moment, he stared at her nakedness, her body now a grown woman's figure. "You are beautiful," he told her, kissing her neck.

Lucrezia opened his doublet and pulled the tucked shirt from his trousers. She sunk back into the thick bed covers as the rest of his heavy clothing thumped to the floor.

Savio's lean body moved beside her. He kissed her for a long moment before his finger slowly ran across the tip of her bare breast. A slight gasp escaped her as the nipple tightened and puckered. Next, his finger drifted to the other breast, circling the rosebud nipple. She moaned and stroked his black hair. Savio's touch was gentle and held much affection. He kissed her deeply, straddling her. The weight of his broad chest carried on his elbows, his mouth and tongue capturing her body's soft mounds and recesses.

Lucrezia gasped at the tingle and rush of new sensations. Her back arched willingly. Everything fell away, but for this single moment, this instance, that brought an ecstasy she had never known. The world hummed and buzzed in a frenzied state. Finally, her hands grasped his hips, urging him forward into her, and he wasted no time. A powerful surge of pleasure kept them in rhythmic motion until the ache overtook everything, and Savio shuddered. They collapsed together, tangled in the covers, holding each other for a long while.

"How is it you have my heart so easily?" Lucrezia finally said. There was a long pause, which grew longer as she waited for an answer.

"Because you have mine, too," Savio replied. "Hearts know."

Tears pricked her eyes for the joy that filled her heart.

***

Lucrezia slipped into Savio's waiting arms from her favorite horse, a spirited stallion with a rich black mane. He helped her from the saddle, holding her about the waist a moment longer than necessary before setting her down. At Lucrezia's invitation, a small riding party had spent most of the brisk fall afternoon exploring Rome's countryside. In addition, a picnic had been arranged close to the palace.

Since Lucrezia's encounter with Savio a few months ago, she had felt alive and in love. She refused to stay shut up in the palace. She longed to be with him, to feel the weight of his body on hers and watch his eyes gleam with desire. The excitement of having Savio in her bed and at her side pulsed through her body as notes plucked from a harp, a sensual song of dizzying attraction that held the promise of love.

Present were two of Lucrezia's newly assigned ladies-in-waiting, giddy sisters, Madelena and Sansia, from a family of distant but noteworthy Borgia cousins. Also attending the ride was Giulia's middle sister, Duchess Girolama Conti, and her reserved husband, Duke Ramon, who had arrived from Umbria for baby Laura's Christening in three days. Girolama rode her white mare side-saddle with a distinct aloofness, her back perfectly erect as if she had other more important things to attend to. Ramon, too, rode beside his wife with apparent indifference. Ramon was a captain of high distinction in the Umbria army who held himself in even higher esteem. Finally, other less significant lords and ladies joined the group, none of whom were of Lucrezia's choosing. The entire entourage had been handpicked by Burchard, who thought Lucrezia's idea to hold a picnic would be an excellent way to entertain the Conti guests. Lucrezia would have preferred, of course, to have Savio all to herself, but she agreed, insisting that Savio be her escort.

The party dismounted and settled onto blankets laid out near the banks of a gentle river. Four wooden posts had secured a billowy white canvas overhead to provide shade. Baskets filled with pork, crusty bread, cheese, and mead vessels welcomed the hungry riders. Sansia distributed the food onto serving platters while Madelena offered drinks.

Girolama arranged her long maroon cape on the blanket and sat precisely as she had on her saddle. In appearance only, she was an older version of Giulia.

Her full lips and creamy complexion were as alluring as her sister's. Yet, unlike Giulia, she was contemplative and dour and frowned upon her sister's relationship with the Pope. The illegitimacy of baby Laura she liked even less. It was easy to read the opinions she tried to hide behind her dark Italian eyes. Nevertheless, Lucrezia did her best to make conversation and keep the mood of the afternoon light and carefree.

"I wish Giulia could have joined us today," Lucrezia said to Girolama.

"My sister is busy planning the Christening celebration for the child," she sniffed, unable to say Laura's name.

"I am sure it will be wonderful. Giulia is gifted with such things," Lucrezia replied cheerfully.

Girolama flicked an insect from her sleeve and made no reply.

Ramon removed his leather riding gloves and accepted a cup from Madelena. "You are a sergeant," he said to Savio, taking a large swallow of wine.

"I am," Savio answered and reached for a cup.

"You battled the French during the failed invasion of Naples," Ramon stated.

"I served under General Juan Borgia, yes, but I am uncertain you could call it a battle," Savio answered.

"What would you call it?" Ramon said, his voice thick with indignation. "General Juan Borgia is a most capable strategist."

"I call it a successful negotiation started by Cesare and his sister." Savio glanced at Lucrezia, the admiration in his eyes unmistakable.

"You suggest Cesare's sister, a woman, convinced the French to negotiate?" Roman exclaimed. "Absurd!"

"Cesare and Lucrezia convinced His Holiness to seek terms even with the balance of her marriage dowry at stake," Savio replied smoothly.

"A dowry that was divided in two and lost," he reminded Savio. One half was gifted to the French, and the other half was lost to the traitorous Sforzas."

Lucrezia's mind raced. She knew Savio was only defending her honor, and she loved him for it, but the conversation was not without hazard. For Savio to challenge a military man who was his senior in rank was dangerous.

"You are too kind," Lucrezia said quickly. "Of course, Juan is a brilliant tactician. It was his idea to negotiate terms. Cesare and I simply endorsed his recommendation. No doubt Juan's intercession saved the lives of many soldiers and civilians on both sides." Her eyes lowered at the weight of Savio's stare. "Juan is intelligent. Of course, using my dowry as leverage was something only Juan would think of."

The surrounding chatter quieted as the picnickers leaned in for a listen, homing in on the uncomfortable turn in the conversation.

Girolama carefully tucked a stray hair back under her feathered riding hat and turned her attention to Savio. "Strange that the palace would select a sergeant as an escort. Would not a foot soldier be a more appropriate choice? Perhaps the sergeant is here for pleasure and not so much protection?"

Lucrezia bristled. "The sergeant is here at my father's insistence. The Pope is keen on our family's protection."

"Do Borgias have many enemies?" Girolama asked pointedly.

Lucrezia raised her chin. She was tired of this woman and her veiled accusations. "We do. Both far and near."

***

Lucrezia had been seeing Savio for almost several months when Juan came to her one evening in her bedchamber full of venom and drink. Pietra was with her as they both worked on their needlepoint. Lucrezia knotted the deep crimson thread and severed the last stitch with her teeth, finally finishing the last of the cherry trees in the colorful pastoral scene.

The visit was inevitable. She had kept Savio away from his soldiering duties too long, requesting him to escort her even when it was unnecessary. She told herself she should have been more cautious, rationing him like fine wine, but the temptation was too great and overtook her thoughts and actions as if they were no longer hers. Then, of course, Savio's absence was noticed.

Her brother lifted a high-backed chair from the corner and set it roughly beside hers. He sat with legs apart, with no sense of manners or etiquette. Mead wafted from his gold-trimmed tunic like sour musk.

"Leave us," Lucrezia told Pietra. The girl swiftly rose, laying her needlepoint aside, and wasted no time exiting the chamber as Juan's lustful stare trailed behind her rounded backside.

"You've been whoring yourself out to my man, Savio," Juan spat, leaning closer.

"I am no whore," she replied calmly, hoping he did not hear the tremor in her voice, "and I don't care for your tone."

Juan closed his hand into a fist, and her breaths quickened, but she raised her chin. Whoring was not what she and Savio shared. The way of wantonness was all Juan knew. He would never understand love, and she refused to accept such a depraved accusation.

"You will stop seeing him," he demanded, leaning closer.

Lucrezia levelled her eyes to his. "I will not."

Without warning, Juan swatted the embroidery from her lap, breaking the round wooden frame as it hit the tiled floor. Her fingers throbbed.

Lucrezia scrambled to retrieve the sewing and ran out of her brother's reach to the fireplace.

Juan rose to his feet, his eyes crazed with anger. "What do you call it, dear Sister, when a woman opens her legs and spreads her cunny for a man?"

"You disgust me!" she cried and turned away.

The blow was hard and unexpected. Lucrezia slammed to the floor, her head thudding against the marble hearth. All went black as the ringing in her ears filled her skull, erasing all other sounds. Before Lucrezia could recover from the assault, Juan jerked her to her feet. Warm blood trickled from a wound on the side of her head. She stumbled forward and stuck out a foot to steady herself.

Juan grabbed her violently by the shoulders. A sadistic smile spread across his face. "That was for laying with Savio. This is for helping Giovanni get away!"

He struck her again, this time a punch to her stomach. Lucrezia realized that where he delivered his blows was intentional. He did not want to mark her face.

Lucrezia fell to her knees. The breath knocked from her body. She felt the urge to vomit, and a sharp pain shot from one of her ribs. She fell forward and curled into a ball, hoping to shield herself from more blows.

The door flew open, and Pietra rushed into the room. "Princess!"

For the first time, Lucrezia was grateful for Pietra's eavesdropping ways. She lifted her head in time to see Juan seize her servant and throw her onto Lucrezia's massive bed. Lucrezia could not see what Juan was doing from the floor, but from Pietra's pleading and shrieks, there was no doubt what was about to happen. Lucrezia heard several loud slaps and then silence.

"Scream again, and I will open your face with my blade!"

Lucrezia tried to stand but could only make it to her knees. She could see Pietra's pale, bare legs and gown hiked up around her waist. Juan forced himself between her thighs, his hips thrusting blindly. The scene resembled two animals rutting, as she had often witnessed on her mother's farm. Her brother's thrusts were brutal and unrelenting until Juan reared his head and released a guttural and incoherent moan. He collapsed upon the girl only for a moment before quickly standing. She heard him clear his throat and spit.

Pietra lay unmoving as Juan quickly dressed and strode past Lucrezia and out the door as if they had all passed an evening of light fare and pleasantries. Lucrezia found her footing and scrambled to the bed. The girl still lay naked from the waist down, her bloodied legs splayed apart. A good deal of blood covered the bedspread under her bottom, and a glob of mucous lay across her stomach.

"Pietra," she whispered gently.

Pietra's eyes stared blankly at the ceiling, blinking out of instinct every few seconds.

Lucrezia moved closer. She had never witnessed such violence, and nausea swiftly gripped her as a gush of blood burst from the girl's private part.

"Pietra!" she said again, this time more forcefully.

The girl turned her head and faced Lucrezia, letting out a soft mew like a wounded animal.

Lucrezia grabbed a small throw blanket and quickly folded it into a thick square. She pressed the fabric between Pietra's legs and braced it in place. "I am sorry. So, so very sorry," Lucrezia repeated as hot tears traveled down her cheeks.

Tears gathered in Pietra's eyes and tumbled down her face into her matted hair. Lucrezia gently placed Pietra's hands on the makeshift bandage. "Hold this," she told her.

Pietra did as instructed, her crying eyes still fixed on the ceiling. After a while, the bleeding slowed and then finally stopped. Lucrezia stroked her servant's cheek until her tears ceased, too. Next, she heated water, soaked a cloth, and gently wiped the blood drying between Pietra's thighs. Finally, when she could sit upright, she drank the wine Lucrezia gave her and allowed Lucrezia to change her torn and soiled gown.

"You are bleeding," Pietra said as Lucrezia laced the dress.

With each breath, a sharp pain stabbed at her side, and her head throbbed from where the blood flowed. Lucrezia found a cloth and dabbed the head wound. At the same time, her mind played out the attack again in vivid detail as she relived the actions of the "creature" she called her brother. A wave of sadness and anger rushed over her. Tears came to her eyes, and her body heaved and shook with the sobs that followed. Pietra reached for her arm and pulled her down next to her on the bed, and together, for a long while, they cried.

After a while, Lucrezia sat up and looked at Pietra. "You must go back to your rooms," she told her. "You cannot stay here in my bed. It will cause suspicion."

Pietra's eyes widened with a storm of worry. "Please don't make me," she begged, throwing her arms around Lucrezia's waist. "You understand not the way of these things!"

"Of what things? Rape? Ravaging another human being for nothing but sadistic pleasure and depravity?"

Over time, from the comfort of her palace carriage, Lucrezia had seen the whores that called to the men on the street, beckoning them to enter their rooms to exchange sex for ducats. She had witnessed men walk through those arched doorways as if innocently purchasing a sack of flour, leather for a coat, or saddle oil. Then there were the victims of rape. A shepherdess bent over a tree while her sheep grazed. A flower vendor pressed against an alley wall with a hand clamped down on her mouth. A milk maiden held down in a barn, her apron soaked with spilled milk, and now a servant girl beaten and taken by force in her mistress' bedchamber. And, of course, a princess made to marry and lay with a man she did not love.

"I wish I could say Juan will be punished, but I cannot."

"He will come back. He will return for me. Take me again and again. He is a dog who takes a bone and

knows where to go for another." Pietra folded her hands
prayerfully. "Please, Princess... I beg you!"

Lucrezia thought for a moment. Pietra was right. And,
besides, Juan's threats against his own sister had escalated
to violence. That violence was sure to continue on his
whim. Perhaps it made sense to stay together. Protect each
other. Either way, Lucrezia silently vowed to stop Juan,
even if it meant erasing him forever from the earth. A
world with one less depraved soul, brother or not, lifted
her broken spirit.

Lucrezia brushed the tears from her wet cheeks,
strangely satisfied. "Very well."

CHAPTER NINE

Giulia held the sick bucket in front of Lucrezia's face, catching last night's roasted pork in choking waves of nausea. "Where is Pietra? This is her duty, not mine!"

Little did Giulia realize Pietra had already held the bucket for hours. The stomach sickness took hold in the middle of the night. When Lucrezia could no longer withstand the agony and felt the knot in her stomach tighten and rise to her throat, she cried for Pietra, who had slept on the floor in her bedchamber ever since the rape. By daybreak, desperate for relief, Lucrezia told Pietra to find a remedy at the apothecary but first to bring Giulia to her.

"Where is that blasted girl!" Giulia cursed.

The week was almost over. Merchants and vendors were busy preparing for the market, the busiest day before stalls and businesses shut down for the Sabbath. Lucrezia knew it would be difficult for Pietra to complete the task quickly. Finally, Pietra arrived carrying a small brown sack tied with a bit of twine, still walking stiffly with a slight limp from Juan's attack a few days ago.

"Stop dawdling," Giulia scolded and grabbed the sack from Pietra's hand. "What did the apothecary say? Did you recite the symptoms the way I told you?"

"Yes, mistress," Pietra replied with hesitation.

"Well, what was his response?"

Pietra twisted her hands nervously and stared at the floor. "He questioned whether ..." her voice dropped to a whisper, "perhaps the Princess is with child?"

Giulia tossed her head back and laughed. "With child? Ridiculous!"

Lucrezia's eyes widened, and her palm immediately touched her stomach. What else could it be? she thought. She had been careful with Giovanni's seed and faithful with Pietra's old family regiment to ward off pregnancy, but she had been careless with Savio. Passion had led her to be inattentive to the fruit of their lovemaking.

"Could this be true?" Giulia gasped.

"Yes," Lucrezia replied, not bothering to argue the point.

The wave of nausea lessened. A strange flutter replaced the sickening stir in Lucrezia's abdomen. Of course, it was too early to feel an infant's movement, and Lucrezia was sure her mind played tricks. Still, she went along with the falsehood because it gave her hope for future things. A whirlwind of emotions flooded her at once. She feared her father's wrath, even though he had bedded many women outside of marriage and flaunted his illegitimate children like a proud peacock. She dared to hope. Perhaps her father would soften to the idea of her marrying Savio despite the man not being of noble birth or providing a desirable family alliance. She imagined Savio's reaction, too. Would he sweep her into his arms, eager to be her husband and loving father to their child, or turn away, feeling saddled by domestic life and the constraints of marriage?

"Who is the father?" Giulia demanded, still reeling from the possibility.

"A soldier."

"A soldier? Have you gone mad?"

"He cares for me, and I for him," Lucrezia answered evenly.

Giulia stared at Lucrezia for a moment, then said, "You think to marry him!"

The astonishment in her voice bordered on anguish, reflecting her elusive marriage to Rodrigo. "It won't happen," she spat, "your father will never allow it!"

Lucrezia bristled at Giulia's tone. Who was she to judge pregnancy out of wedlock, considering her situation?

"I am a grown woman and will make my own decisions," Lucrezia replied. "Besides, no man will have me now, not with another man's child."

"You are still a Borgia!" Giulia gathered her skirts in a rush to leave. "I will send for the royal surgeon to see if the apothecary is correct, and if he is, I will tell your father. Then we shall see the extent of Rodrigo's compassion," Giulia said gleefully.

"Do that," Lucrezia countered. "If I am with child, it is mine to keep. My father will have no say in the matter."

Giulia made no answer but slammed the door in a rage as she left.

Pietra sunk to her knees and covered her face with her hands. "I am sorry, Princess. I had to tell the truth. The apothecary knew right away when I explained your illness."

Lucrezia gently touched the top of the servant girl's head. "Hush now. The truth will eventually have made itself known. I am not angry, and I am not sad. I shall face my father, and he will come to terms with the reality of the situation."

"There is another reality you must consider," Pietra said, raising her head. Dark shadows circled her eyes. "When Juan learns the truth, he will be furious."

Lucrezia twisted her soiled nightdress in her lap. Pietra was right. Of course, Juan would be furious. More than furious, murderous perhaps. Lucrezia's condition would

be a black mark against Juan as a commander and a Borgia.
Rodrigo may even question his ability to lead. After all,
how could Juan possibly control an army when one of
his soldiers impregnated his sister? Then, a dark thought
made her heart skip. Juan may beat her again to make
her miscarry. Lucrezia was astonished the pregnancy had
survived the beating from a few days ago. Suddenly, she
feared Juan more than Rodrigo.

"I must be ready for him," Lucrezia said. "Ready for his
wrath."

Pietra slowly stood and reached for a satchel hidden
beneath her apron. She untied the thin string and pulled
out a flask no bigger than a fig. It was black and plugged at
the opening with the slightest bit of cork.

Lucrezia took it from Pietra and turned it over in her
hands. "What is this?"

"Cantarella."

"Poison?"

Pietra nodded and stared at her feet.

For a moment, the thought of what Pietra proposed
shocked her. Lucrezia held in her hands the means of
murdering her brother. But she also had the means to
secure the safety of her baby.

"You bought this from the apothecary?" Lucrezia asked,
knowing that there would be a record of the purchase.

"I lifted it from behind the counter while the apprentice
prepared your remedy."

"You stole it," Lucrezia said, faintly relieved. "How do you know of it?"

"In Palermo, where I am from, there was an old vagrant woman who peddled flowers to the villagers. She also sold poison to unhappy wives. My mother was a good woman but an unhappy wife," Pietra replied in a neutral tone.

"How does it work?" Lucrezia asked and touched the cork with her fingertip.

"Careful, Princess," Pietra warned. "It is a potent powder. Just a pinch mixed with wine will drop a man instantly. He will be dead within minutes.

"And you are sure he cannot be saved? There is no antidote?"

"Some say eating charcoal can save you if taken in time, but the poison works swiftly. My father foamed at the mouth. Blood seeped from his ears and eyes. My brother ran for the surgeon, but it was too late. My father was crazed and choked to death on his vomit." Pietra shrugged her shoulders. "The man had many enemies. So no one pursued the matter."

Lucrezia recoiled at how measured the girl recounted the violent death of her father. The man must have made Pietra's mother a most unhappy wife. Juan had enemies. Lucrezia was sure of it. And her father would pursue Juan's murder. So, the plan had to be flawless.

"Juan keeps a wine vessel on the table in his bedchamber. He drinks most of it every night to help him sleep. I shall taint the wine with this Cantarella."

Pietra shook her head vehemently. "No, Princess, there is too much risk. I will carry out the deed."

Lucrezia pulled Pietra to her feet and stared straight into the girl's mournful eyes. "He is my brother, and as your father made your mother an unhappy wife, my brother has made me a very unhappy sister."

***

Rodrigo's wrath was usually a blustery inferno of biting rage, swift and unyielding. Still, Rodrigo did not send for Lucrezia immediately after the royal surgeon confirmed her pregnancy. He did not send for her the next day either. Three days passed before her father summoned her to his papal chamber. The Swiss Guards posted outside the massive chamber door allowed her entrance. She found Rodrigo seated at a desk in his formal parlor, reading from a large manuscript bound in black cloth.

Lucrezia stood in front of him, waiting to be recognized. Several minutes ticked by before he glanced up from the book and removed his silver reading spectacles. He waved to an empty chair, and she sat down, unable to read his thoughts from his neutral expression. It was not what she expected.

Without Burchard's usual presence, she was alone with her father. The same man who playfully chased her among the winding paths of Vannozza's villa when she was a child held once more the power to manage her fate and decide her destiny. That little girl seemed a distant memory now as Lucrezia sat before him straight-backed and ready for the fight to begin.

Suddenly coming to life, Rodrigo patted the thick black book before him. "Do you know what this is?" His voice was calm and unassuming.

Lucrezia stared at the manuscript and shook her head. She had never seen it before.

"This book is the Sacred Articles of the Carmelites," he said, casually flipping through the first few pages. "The Carmelite nuns are dedicated to poverty, chastity, obedience, and contemplation. They are a cloistered order, focused on quiet prayer and reflection, and rarely leave their abbey. You will take this book and learn it."

"Why am I to know this?" Lucrezia asked stiffly.

Rodrigo slammed his fist hard on the marble table, sending a jolt through Lucrezia's spine. "You will be confined with the Carmelites until this unpleasant situation is over! You will spend hours on your knees praying to our Lord and the Blessed Virgin Mother for forgiveness."

"I will not!"

"You will!" Rodrigo seethed. The anger she had expected boiled over. "If the child is female, she will remain there, dedicating her life to solitude and prayer, and it will save her soul. A male child will go to the priory at Messina to live among the monks, and he shall be saved."

"My child shall never take holy orders!"

Rodrigo leaned back in his chair and crossed his arms. "Would you rather I let Juan handle the matter?"

"You wouldn't!"

"I would. As it stands, your temperamental brother is quite busy searching for the child's father, the soldier Savio. He has suddenly disappeared."

The blood drained from Lucrezia's face, and the room swirled like a tidepool. Her faithful Pietra must have warned him.

"If Juan were to find this man you care for, you would want him to remain," Rodrigo paused, "... alive? Therefore, I believe it is in your best interest and the interest of your Savio that you do as I ask."

Lucrezia nodded silently. Tears stained her cheeks. She had failed her unborn child. She had failed to stand up to her father. The only thing left was to pray for Savio to remain safe.

***

Mother Lucia swung open the door to Lucrezia's cell to find her bed unmade - again. The woman, dressed in long layers of heavy woolen fabric, frowned and shook her head. A series of veils of varying lengths framed her slim, pale face, the final one covering her neck and shoulders.

"Here, you are not the Pope's daughter at our abbey. Within these walls, while you remain with us, you will obey the Articles of Order," the wrinkled-faced woman commanded, as she had done every morning since Lucrezia's arrival eight long months ago.

Lucrezia stood in her nightdress, cupping her rounded stomach, and said nothing.

Mother Lucia clucked her tongue and left.

No punishment was handed down to Lucrezia and her flagrant disregard for the elderly abbess' rules. Maybe she was still, in some small way, Pope Alexander VI's daughter.

Each nun had a windowless cell at the abbey, containing a bed, a desk, a chair, and a crucifix centered on an otherwise blank wall. Convent life was a stark contrast to the vibrant colors and decadence of the Vatican. The walls surrounding Lucrezia were a colorless portrait set upon a backdrop of monotonous whitewash. The abbey at Messina was a short distance from its neighboring priory, which housed an order of Franciscan monks. A secure stone wall kept the two estates separate except for frequent meetings between Mother Lucia and Abbott

Rinaldo. The Carmelite complex contained a modest church, the convent which housed the nunnery, a series of outbuildings used for farming, and an infirmary for serving the sick and needy.

Her door opened again. This time, Sister Lorena entered, smiled, pulled the blankets over the bed, and fluffed the hard pillow as best she could. The nun was a novice and had yet to take her final vows. Nevertheless, she was a cheerful girl, not much older than Lucrezia, with a creamy complexion and light hazel eyes. Lucrezia guessed the girl's hair was probably reddish and closely cropped under her gray habit.

"How do you feel today?" the young girl asked pleasantly.

"Bored and tired. No different from yesterday," Lucrezia replied.

"You must tell me the minute you feel the pangs," Sister Lorena said. "Mother Lucia wants to know immediately."

"Then what?" Lucrezia asked.

"I am not privy to such information." The girl folded a woolen blanket and laid it neatly on the bed.

"You won't keep my baby," Lucrezia replied bluntly. "I am the baby's mother. The child is mine no matter what my father plans."

Lorena bowed her head and made the sign of the cross. "You are in my prayers daily, Princess."

The nun was the only Carmelite who called Lucrezia by her royal title, even curtsied if the abbess was not looking, perhaps captivated in the presence of an actual princess. "Your child will be safe at either our abbey or the priory. I am sure of it," she continued. "The babe will be well taught and cared for, living a life dedicated to our Lord and Savior."

"Is that what you wanted for yourself?" Lucrezia asked pointedly. "Live in seclusion from the world and all its beauty? Do you not wish for someone to satiate your womanly appetite? That longing to forge two beings into one? To act on the desire and feeling of sharing this life with someone else? How can you stand it? This suffocation of spirit? Your spirit?"

If Lucrezia's words wounded the girl, she did not show it. Instead, Lorena reached under the bed for the chamber pot, which Lucrezia was directed to empty each morning.

The young nun turned to Lucrezia. "My family works a small farm on rented land. They return most of their income to Lord Baccio of Messina, who rents it from the church. I am one of ten children, seven boys and three girls. My family is impoverished. The men farm the fields, and my mother earns extra coin as a weaver." She cradled the pot as if it were an infant. "My two younger sisters died of the fever last winter. As I was our landowner's property, Lord Baccio gave me to the abbey. He told my parents I would be better off serving the poor of Messina, and they would be better off with one less mouth to feed. Perhaps he did not wish to pay for another burial."

"What did your parents say?" Lucrezia asked.

Lorena shrugged. "What could they say? He was right."

"How do you know he was right?" Lucrezia challenged. "You have nothing to compare this life with. You have never even been with a man."

"I am fed and clothed. In return, I feed the hungry and tend to the sick. Some things in this world are more important than romantic dalliances. Sometimes, the greater good is more significant than the needs of just one lowly farm girl."

***

"Bear down!" Lorena pleaded and mopped Lucrezia's brow with a cold cloth.

Childbirth had gripped Lucrezia suddenly one evening during Vespers. Mild phantom pangs had begun a few days earlier. Although Mother Lucia allowed Lucrezia to continue ladling soup to the hungry, Lucrezia knew they watched her closely.

There was no time to move Lucrezia. The old abbess ordered a makeshift bed be made in the nave's corner by securing wooden benches together. Blankets and clean linen arrived, along with a jug of wine and hot water.

Legs spread, propped up on her elbows, Lucrezia could make out Jesus dying on the cross to the left of one of the infirmary nuns hovering over her. She had never witnessed a crucifixion but guessed it could not be worse than the babe splitting her in half.

The pain came in waves, starting slowly, mounting and swelling until the agony came crashing down, only to begin again and again. Time refused to move forward or back but remained stuck in one tortuous present. Then, finally, Lucrezia felt a hand press against her swollen private part.

"It's time," Mother Lucia announced.

Lorena whispered in her ear. "When the next pang comes, you must push, push, push like never before."

In another life, Lucrezia would have questioned how the young novice knew such things, but she did as she was told. When the next surge came, she pushed with all her strength. This time, the pain came with enormous pressure.

"Get her up!" Mother Lucia commanded Lorena, who stood in awe at what was unfolding. "Hurry, you fool!"

Hands reached beneath Lucrezia's shoulders and hoisted her, almost folding her in half.

The pain and the pressure were unbearable, but something was moving through her, opening and sliding out. Except for a fiery burning between her legs, the agony diminished. The old nun turned away, and several other sisters swarmed around her. A flurry of excitement enveloped the room.

A high-pitched wail pierced the air.

"It is a male," Sister Lucia announced.

Lucrezia fought to keep her eyes open. Through a blur, she could make out Lorena next to Mother Lucia. But Lorena did not focus on the wailing bundle cradled by the abbess. Lorena's eyes were wide with terror, staring at Lucrezia's sprawled legs. "Blood ...so much blood," the young novice said before collapsing on the cold church floor.

CHAPTER TEN

Lucrezia opened her eyes. A familiar whitewashed ceiling and rough-cut beam appeared above her. She was back in her tiny cell at the nunnery. Someone had replaced her clothes with a plain gray shift. A heavy wool blanket covered her body. Lucrezia felt beneath the thick wool and found a warm compress across her swollen stomach. They told her she had birthed a boy. But where was he? The last thing she remembered was Mother Lucia holding him, and then—nothing. Fear and confusion gripped her. Had the babe been removed from the abbey already?

Lucrezia abruptly sat up in bed despite the stabbing pain between her legs. Her hand felt again under the cover, and her fingers touched the spiny knots of stitches inside her private part. She searched the cell for a cradle, but there was none.

The arched door swung open, and Lorena and Mother Lucia entered. Lorena carried a steaming mug that smelled of warm ale.

"Where is my baby?" Lucrezia snapped.

"With a wet nurse," the old nun answered sharply.

"I demand to see him!"

"You are in no position to make demands," Mother Lucia replied. You should be grateful for Sister Margarite's quick attention. She saved your life."

"You almost bled out," Lorena solemnly added. "Many novenas were said on your behalf throughout the night."

"The babe is healthy and being properly cared for. Now, you must let us do the same for you. Rest and regain your strength so you may return to the Papal Palace. We must keep the Pope's intention at heart."

"His intention is cruel and unnatural and will never be forgiven!" Lucrezia spat.

Mother Lucia placed her hand on the young novice's shoulder. "Stay with her. Be sure she rests and stays in her cell." She looked back at Lucrezia with a clear warning in her stern eyes before leaving.

Lucrezia swallowed the urge to tell the old abbess that her baby would be hers no matter what her father ordained. However, being combative now would only encourage the woman to be more vigilant, making escape especially difficult.

Lorena waited until the door was closed before settling beside Lucrezia on the bed. Lucrezia hid her resentment at the girl's familiarity. Becoming estranged from the one person who showed her kindness would be a mistake.

Lorena handed her the ale. "Drink."

Despite Lucrezia's ill feelings towards the novice, she drank the cup heartily. The ale was warm and welcome in her empty stomach. Her body ached with the pain of childbirth and the absence of a baby she longed to hold.

"Thank you," Lucrezia said, handing her the empty cup.

"You will be well in no time," Lorena said. She placed the cup on the floor, opened the satchel strapped across her shoulder, and began pulling out yards of fabric cut into long strips.

"What are those for?" Lucrezia said.

"To bind your breasts. The pressure will help dry your milk."

Lucrezia's eyes widened in horror. "I forbid it!"

"Without nursing, your breasts will become engorged. They will ache terribly before they dry up, so I've been told. Binding them will hurry along the inevitable," Lorena explained.

"I must nurse my babe, not a wet nurse. It is my duty."

Lorena stiffened. "As it is my duty to bind you." She moved to help Lucrezia sit up further, which Lucrezia

obliged. Still, when the young novice reached to remove
the shift to expose her breasts, Lucrezia swatted her away,
snatched the mound of wool, and hurled it against the far
wall.

"You will not do this!" Lucrezia seethed. "At least let me
keep my milk!" Her eyes filled with angry tears. "I care not
if doing so causes me pain. It can be no more painful than
denying a mother her son."

A shadow crossed Lorena's pale cheeks, and she stood
silent and rooted to the cold stone floor for a few peculiar
moments. Finally, without words, she turned and left,
quietly closing the door behind her.

Lorena was correct. Lucrezia's breasts did ache and
throb. Hours passed before the door opened again, and
Lorena returned. In her arms was the same satchel, and
Lucrezia braced herself for another attempt at binding
her breasts. But as she approached Lucrezia's bed, an
unmistakable cooing came from inside the rounded
pouch.

"Shush, little one," Lorena said softly. She carefully
scooped up the tiny babe and gently placed him in
Lucrezia's unsteady arms. We must be quiet," she warned.
I sent the wet nurse off to rest. Mother Lucia will be
furious if we are found out."

Lucrezia's heart flooded with joy and astonishment that
the young novice would take such a risk on her behalf.
Lorena's warning was not lost on her. The girl's life as a

nun would be finished if the old abbess entered the room. As Lucrezia peered down at her new son and his soft cap of black hair and dark eyes, her world stopped. Every feature reminded her of Savio. She wished for her lover to be with them at this precious moment. Lucrezia held the babe closer, lifting his head to her lips. "You shall know your father one day," she vowed, her voice a whisper. "I must name you," she suddenly realized. "You cannot leave my side again without knowing your name."

The idea of naming the child "Savio" was her first thought, but it was fleeting. There could not be any link between the man her father sought to punish and this innocent babe. So, the designation had to be clever. The name must bewitch her father into keeping the child close to him and, in that way, close to her.

"His name shall be Rodrigo," she told Lorena. "It is my father's given name, the man I loved as a child before he became Pope and I became a forsaken princess. Remember that in case anything should happen to me."

"Nothing will happen to you," Lorena answered in a steady voice, words slow and deliberate. "You are leaving tonight, Princess. You and your child."

Lucrezia turned her gaze from the babe to the young novice, thinking the girl had misspoken. "What are you saying? How can you promise anything?"

"I have not been candid with you, Princess," Lorena said, lowering her eyes. Lord Baccio brought me to this

place, but not to lessen his burden. But, like you, I was with
a child."

"With child?"

"Lord Baccio's child."

"He raped you?" Lucrezia's voice quivered, and her
mind swirled with the memory of Pietra and Juan's violent
assault.

Lorena continued with vacant eyes. "The lord
discovered I had a lover. He beat me and cursed me for
being a girl of low morals. He said since I was a whore, I
should be his whore as well." Lorena jutted her chin. "I
am no whore," she said with anger. "Never did I lie with a
man before Raul. I swear."

"Of course, there is no need to explain," Lucrezia replied
softly. Still, to her dismay, the acknowledgment did not
halt Lorena from telling her tale.

"Raul's family were traveling stonecutters from
Palermo, hired by our landlord to create an outbuilding
for our pigs," Lorena recounted, as if in a trance.

Lucrezia wanted to press her hands to her head, prevent
the words from reaching her ears, sure that the story
to follow would be a heart-wrenching remembrance.
She wished nothing more than to take back her earlier
admonishment of the girl's situation at the nunnery and
her accusation of a life not fulfilled. Instead, Lucrezia's
cheeks flushed with shame.

Lorena pressed her hands over her heart. "We met secretly every evening after our families supped. Our mothers exchanged niceties over the price of wheat and how best to store grain. Our fathers discussed limestone and water for mud and how to grow hay. For many nights, Raul and I reveled in that same hay, his hands touching me in places I never dared to touch myself."

Lucrezia listened without interruption, knowing there was no stopping the floodgate of emotion.

"So, yes, Princess," Lorena continued. "I know the touch of man and his presence inside me. I understand your pain of love lost. You may not see it, but I have a constant storm swirling down deep. It disturbs my sleep and chokes my dreams until I awaken to a new day of doing Mother Lucia's bidding. And what of God, you may ask? Why did He not show me solace during my darkest days? In my quest to be his obedient servant, I asked myself those questions, too. Where was He in all my pain, in all my suffering?" Lorena moved to Lucrezia's side and clutched her hand. "Perhaps it was all to bring me to you."

She stared strangely at the novice nun. How could they share a moment so intimate yet live lives so far apart? Did they not watch the same leaf change from green to burnt orange? Did they not foresee the same leaf falling dead to the ground only to fertilize the earth come spring? Did they not observe the same ice-driven wind make frigid water become frozen? Did they not deeply breathe the earthy smell of spring soil, revel in the hot summer bounty, and feast in the season hunt? They did not. They did none of that. Despite being worlds apart, they clung to each other like dying leaves on a vine. They were as different as the moon and the sun, rising and setting apart. Their lives hung in the same universe. Yet they never connected. They only knew each other just now. They were mothers and creators of life. They birthed children into the same world who breathed the same air and opened their eyes with the same innocence and wonder. That made them equal.

Lucrezia squeezed Lorena's hand just as forcefully. "I am unworthy of such a friendship," she said, choking back tears.

Lorena caressed the newly named Rodrigo's head. "I know not of what happened to my baby daughter. Lord Baccio probably rid himself of her, too, given she would be no help as a farmhand."

"Why was she not sent here with you?" Lucrezia asked.

"A wayward woman cannot just appear at the convent gate and expect to be taken in, especially with an infant... unless you are the Pope's daughter, of course," Lorena added. "Money must change hands. Sometimes what Mother Lucia demands is hefty, and Lord Baccio was most likely in no position to pay for us both."

"Can you not seek her out?"

"I have searched to no avail. Perhaps it is best this way. I have no means to support myself or a child."

Lucrezia stared at the girl solemnly. "I do," Lucrezia said. "I will help."

A hopeful flicker crossed the young girl's face as she stared longingly at Rodrigo, but it swiftly vanished. "At this moment, I must help you escape with your son. Deliver you to safety, away from the watchful eyes of Mother Lucia, who will abide by your father's wishes to gain favor and secure a wealthy endowment."

"Very well," Lucrezia said. "I am at your mercy."

Lorena, the young novice who had let her heart bleed to speak the truth about her past, stared back at Lucrezia with emboldened eyes. "You are at no one's mercy," she said. "We must help each other. I can get us out, but you must show the way from there. Can you trust anyone in this undertaking? Is there anyone who can provide us safety?"

Lucrezia stared back without blinking, confident in her choice. "Vannozza dei Cattanei, my mother."

***

That evening, Lorena returned with two laundress baskets made of woven straw. Once the nuns had retired for Vespers, she had successfully wrangled the child away from the wet nurse again. The fat nurse gave Lorena no trouble. She shuffled to the kitchen, content with the promise of stewed lamb. Mother Lucia excused Lorena from the

nightly Mass to tend to Lucrezia, who greeted Lorena,
already dressed in the black robe and nun's habit left
earlier.

"Like this," Lorena said, tucking a stray hair beneath the
thick wool and pulling it down to cover more of Lucrezia's
smooth forehead.

Rodrigo slumbered comfortably in a basket. He slept
soundly, fresh off the plump breast of the wet nurse.
Lorena handed the basket containing the child to
Lucrezia. "Come."

The twosome walked side by side. Eyes turned
downward as most nuns did, Lucrezia kept herself
erect and determined with the same pious gait as her
counterpart. The halls were empty of the usual bustle as
the clanging church bell announced the start of Vespers.

They exited the dormitory and crossed the open
courtyard until they reached the high, stone-walled
boundary of the convent, which encircled the estate's
inner buildings and divided it from the priory. The wall
was high and, in many places, covered in dense ivy.

Sunset had long passed, and the silver-gray of dusk
descended upon them. The women traveled the perimeter
until Lorena suddenly stopped. She buried her hand inside
a patch of thick vines, and with a hard push, a small arched
door opened. Lorena pulled her along, and as they went
through the tiny entrance, Lucrezia found herself inside
the neighboring priory.

"You have done this before," Lucrezia said, keeping her voice low.

"There is a secret trade between the monks and nuns," Lorena replied. "They make communion wine and give us an allotment every week. In return, we sneak them sweets and baked goods. Some unscrupulous nuns sneak them more than that," she admitted with disgust, "but it is mostly a peaceful arrangement."

The priory was laid out much like the convent but more expansive. Like the convent, shrubbery divided the grounds into four sections across the middle courtyard to replicate the holy cross. The refectory, or dining hall, was twice as large as its neighbor's. Lorena told her that the monks educated the wealthy children there. There was a library that served as a place for the tedious task of copying the words of the prophets for safekeeping.

A monk pumping water noticed them, glanced around nervously, and then hurried to them, leaving the bucket behind.

"Brother Ernesto," Lorena said. She folded her hands prayerfully and nodded her head. A sideways glance from Lorena gave Lucrezia a silent nudge to do the same.

The priory church took up a vast corner of the religious fortress. As Lucrezia glanced up at the soaring arched windows and panes of stained glass, she heard the familiar tolling of the church bell summoning the monks to Vespers.

"What do you want?" the old monk asked hastily. Pox marks covered his sunken cheeks.

"I wish to see Friar Dominic," Lorena said.

"He leaves for Florence in the morning," Ernesto snapped. "The good friar has no time for dalliances, and I have no time to do your bidding. You make me tardy for evening prayer."

Friar Dominic visited the priory regularly, peddling goods from neighboring villages for food and religious relics doled out to impoverished peasants and lepers.

"We bring fresh bread for his journey," Lorena said, gesturing at her basket. "Still warm."

"Give it to me," the monk said. "I shall see he gets it."

"So you can steal it for yourself?" Lorena exclaimed. "I think not!" She pulled back the cloth covering the basket top and pulled out a loaf of crusty bread. "Here," she said, "for your trouble. If you do not double-cross me, you will receive two more loaves tomorrow."

The monk held the bread to his pointy nose and breathed deeply, taking in the intoxicating scent of fresh bread. "Wait here," he said and hurried away.

"Sister Oleanna's bread is difficult to resist," Lorena whispered gratefully.

"Who is this Friar Dominic?" Lucrezia asked.

Lorena quickly explained the friar's unique position. "Dominic is our only contact with the outside world. Since he can come and go as he pleases, he takes pity on us and will deliver a message to a dying mother or comfort a jailed father. I pray he helps us. He helped me once before," she said, her voice trailing off.

Lucrezia resisted the urge to question Lorena further. Time did not allow the luxury, and since the girl had trusted the monk in the past, it was enough for her to trust him, too.

Moments later, a dark, hooded shadow moved swiftly across the courtyard. Lucrezia's stomach clenched with fear as she prayed the situation was not a trap. Would the friar seize Rodrigo and drag them back to the nunnery to await Mother Lucia's wrath?

But the hooded man approached with familiarity, embracing Lorena as a brother would a sister. He tossed back his hood, revealing a mound of black curls and a kind, pleasing face. "Sister Lorena," he said, "what brings you at this late hour? I leave for Florence in the morn."

"We need your help," Lorena said, not wasting time. However, Lucrezia quickly noted the sudden blush of crimson on the girl's cheeks.

Friar Dominic raised an eyebrow. "Help?"

Lorena reached for Lucrezia's basket and lifted the corner of the blanket, exposing the sleeping Rodrigo. "This woman and child are in danger. We need safe passage to Rome, to the farm of Vannozza dei Cattanei."

The friar looked at Lucrezia. "What is your name?

"Lucrezia Borgia, daughter of Pope Alexander VI," she answered defiantly.

His expression displayed a mix of shock and curiosity. "We well know of your stay at the convent, and your situation is unfortunate, but I cannot go against the Vicar of the Church," he said, shaking his head.

"The Vicar of the Church is not God," Lucrezia replied angrily.

"He is God's hand here on earth."

"My father intends to keep my son in this place forever, to live among the monks. He demands that I return to the Vatican and never see my child again. I am his mother. He has no right."

Dominic thought for a moment. "A father and his daughter should not be at odds, even if he is Pope. If I help you, promise me you will restore harmony between you and your father. It is the only way."

Lucrezia folded her hands prayerfully and bowed as Lorena had taught. "I agree to return to the Vatican and make peace with my father." She tried not to laugh as she recited the silly lie. Unfortunately, peace with her father was as elusive as his love.

"Very well," he said and made the sign of the cross.

Dominic hurried the women across the courtyard to the front gate. A wagon attached to a mule awaited.

"Get in and keep quiet," the monk said, lifting the canvas. "When we have reached the village outskirts, you may show yourselves. If anyone questions your presence, say you are on a pilgrimage to aid the lepers."

They obliged Dominic's wishes and hid beneath the heavy cloth among the crocks of holy oil, bags of wooden crosses, and baskets of vegetables. The wagon wheels creaked from the extra weight as Dominic urged the mule forward. Lucrezia used the opportunity to feed Rodrigo.

"Did you mean what you said?" Lorena whispered as Rodrigo greedily sucked Lucrezia's breast.

Lucrezia's eyes did not waver. "My father will accept Rodrigo as my child, or there will be no peace."

***

Vannozza's farm was as Lucrezia had left it so long ago after her wedding night with Giovanni, full of bustling life and excitement. Eager farmhands reloaded the market wagons in the lively courtyard. Barrels of olive oil and grain were packed high into carriages to be peddled again in the morning.

Lucrezia's mother received the tired travelers in the expansive, formal garden. Twisted vines of red grapes created a canopy providing shade from the late afternoon sun. Platters of cold meat, bread, and cheese covered the table, along with great jugs of wine. Vannozza swooped into the garden courtyard wearing a pale blue work dress

and linen smock, her hair twisted in a tight braid on top
of her head. She hugged her daughter in a fierce embrace,
and Lucrezia made quick introductions.

"You are not only a woman now but a mother, too,"
Vannozza said, cupping Lucrezia's face with her hands. "I
pray you only know the joy of motherhood and not the
pain I have suffered by your father." She lifted Rodrigo
from his cradle and looked longingly at his sleeping face
before gently kissing his tiny hand. "You were right coming
to me," she continued, still entranced by her grandson. "I
will keep you both safe."

Dominic took a long draft of wine and said, "Lucrezia
has promised to return to the palace and make amends
with her father."

Vannozza shot the friar a stern look. "You shall call her
'Princess!'" Vannozza seethed. "I trust no man of the cloth.
I let you eat my cheese and drink my wine because you
served my daughter and her child, but never forget where
I stand."

"I beg forgiveness," the friar answered, not sounding
like he begged for anything, but bowed his head and
touched his chest with his fist.

"Of what does he speak?" Vannozza asked Lucrezia.
"What is this vulgar promise?"

Lucrezia steadied herself and recited the explanation she
had committed to memory during the journey to the farm.
"I must claim my son's place at the palace, Mother. He is

a Borgia. He will not live in a priory, nor can I hide him within these walls for the rest of his life. Your grandson is a prince of the church and shall live like a prince."

"Your 'dear' father will make this sweet babe do his bidding. Use him as a pawn as he does you. Is that what you want?" her mother spat.

The words stung. What Vannozza uttered held much truth, but Lucrezia kept calm as she answered, "Motherhood brings great responsibly and sometimes hardship. You are my greatest example. There will be joy and sorrow in this world, but a mother's love is endless. You would do no less for me."

Vannozza narrowed her eyes and shifted the subject. "While you embark on this fruitless endeavor, l insist you leave Rodrigo in my safekeeping," she said, "Do that for me."

"Very well," Lucrezia replied, knowing that if she was unsuccessful, at least Rodrigo would be safe.

Later that evening, Lucrezia placed Rodrigo in the cradle beside her bed. The bedchamber, with its large windows, heavy curtains, and fireplace, was far more luxurious than her former convent cell. Earlier, servants had carried in another bed for Lorena. Lucrezia felt the need to keep the girl close after all they had endured together, and besides, she had grown fond of the wayward novice.

"Dominic wishes to take me into the village tomorrow. He is familiar with the market. I can buy new clothes there," Lorena said, spreading a blanket across her bed.

"You like him," Lucrezia teased.

Lorena shrugged. "He interests me," she admitted.

"You mentioned he helped you once. What did he do?"

"Dominic helped search for my baby girl. He made inquiries during his travels. I was distraught. The gesture brought me comfort, although his effort was fruitless."

Lorena slipped beneath the clean, white coverlet. Freedom was perhaps more precious than loyalty, and Lucrezia wondered about Lorena's future.

"What will you do now?" Lucrezia asked.

"Move on. I thought my days as a nun would bring me peace. Instead, seeing you and little Rodrigo forced me to face my pain. There will be no peace for me without my child. She is alone in a world that is cold and unforgiving. She would be about a year old now, and I pray Dominic will help me search for her again," she answered, "if he will have me. Then, with God's mercy, I will find her."

The handsome friar's attraction to the former novice was unmistakable on the journey to her mother's farm. The trip had been uneventful. Only a few times did weary peasants stop them along the road, begging for food. Still, when they approached Lorena, Dominic was never far from her side.

Lucrezia stared at the bedchamber ceiling, covered in a swirl of painted clouds and cherubs. The thought of Lorena leaving brought her unexpected sorrow, but she understood. "I shall miss you," she said after a long moment.

"And I you," Lorena replied softly.

Lucrezia sat up and placed her hand over her heart. "I will never forget the risks you took for me. How you helped us. Know that I will do the same for you. I will do everything in my power to find your babe."

As the words left her mouth, Lucrezia wondered if they held any truth. What power had she wielded thus far? Savio was gone, maybe even dead, and she had been powerless to save him. Tears sprung to her eyes as the sadness of his absence and the love she still felt gripped her again. Lucrezia forced back the tears and swallowed hard as a sudden resolve filled her with determination. The evil perpetrated on Savio and Lorena would meet with vengeance and justice. Fate had finally given her purpose.

CHAPTER ELEVEN

Lucrezia sat in her father's library with her hands folded neatly on her lap. The last time she had seen her father, he banished her to the Carmelites and told her the babe inside her womb would be raised by a religious order. But he was wrong. She had defied him, her father, the man ordained by God to reign the earth in His stead. In fighting him, had she defied God, too? Perhaps her destiny lay in the fiery pits of hell, to burn for all eternity with the rest of the Godless sinners. Lucrezia swallowed hard. Pope Alexander linked his hands behind his back and turned his gaze from the window to his wayward daughter. The glare of his eyes pierced her heart.

"The bastard child is a boy, I am told," Rodrigo said.

Lucrezia raised her chin. "His name is Rodrigo Borgia II, named for you, his grandfather."

Rodrigo grunted. "And you think that will save him?"

"He is a prince of the church. No more, no less than Juan or Cesare or little Geoffre."

"They are my sons!" Rodrigo seethed.

"My son is of your blood, as well," Lucrezia countered. "Your power pulses through his veins. He is a Borgia. By acknowledging that truth, we grow our family. We grow in strength."

Rodrigo paced back and forth a few times. Finally, his brows furrowed over his eyes in deep contemplation. "You must marry again," he said. "No one will marry an impure woman. The child cannot stay, no matter what his name is. It is impossible."

Lucrezia thought hard, her mind frantic for an answer. The future of her son hung in this one moment. "Bring your grandson to the palace. Parade him as Cesare's illegitimate son. The child will remain in my care as Cesare's dutiful sister," Lucrezia posed. The proposition was far from outlandish. Besides her father, men of the cloth often kept mistresses, even setting up a household with them and their bastard children. How could her father deny Cesare the same arrangement, even if the scenario was untrue?

She had not seen either brother since her return. Cesare had sent word promising to dine with her that evening.

Gratefully and relieved, she learned Juan was away spying on the heretics in Florence. A wayward Dominican monk had riled up the populace. The reform movement of Girolamo Savonarola was well-known across the country and only growing in strength. He dared to declare Pope Alexander the devil incarnate. He bellowed from the pulpit that the Pope's lifestyle was too lavish and that church leaders writhed in the pit of golden ore, prostitutes of the coin.

Eager to crack the whip, Rodrigo dispatched Juan and a small legion of soldiers to put down the growing uprising. Yet, Cesare had been held back, his red-caped Cardinal duties too essential to spare. Knowing the circumstance already riled and provoked Cesare, she worried her proposal to claim the babe as his child would also anger him.

Her father's face remained expressionless, then his lips spread into a wry grin, and the gleam in his eye suggested his opinion of her had changed. "You are a clever one, Lucrezia," he said. "Perhaps I underestimated you. What you pose may work, and you will marry again unhindered." Her father rubbed his chin in deep thought. "It shall be done, but never forget I am your father and Pope Alexander VI. Your bastard can disappear just as swiftly as he appeared. Do not cross me again.

***

Lucrezia hurried from her bedchamber window down to the courtyard. The carriage carrying her son had entered the palace gate. Pietra followed closely behind with a receiving blanket to keep the morning chill off little Rodrigo. She desperately wanted to ask Pietra about Savio, but since Lucrezia's return as a royal princess, the attention that flooded her kept the opportunity impossible. The reunion between the two women had been joyous, and Pietra assured Lucrezia that Juan had posed no threat during her absence. Still, Lucrezia feared the bruising on the girl's arm told a different story.

"You are a mother now," Pietra had said. Her bright eyes traced Lucrezia's face as if the visage was somehow now different.

The reunion with Giulia was not as pleasant. The Pope's mistress did not warm to the idea of two royal babes in the palace. Lucrezia vowed to be extra vigilant around Giulia and Juan upon his return. She understood now the power of motherhood—the desire for a child to survive and thrive and the lengths a mother might extend herself to further her offspring's position.

Baby Laura and little Rodrigo may be cousins. Still, Lucrezia could foresee their futures as rivals, vying for the Pope's attention. Both children were illegitimate, but her son was a male, which gave him a more significant standing, likely making Giulia even more unsettled.

Once they reached the back staircase and away from curious ears, Lucrezia stopped and whispered to Pietra. "Where is my Savio? Have you any news?"

Pietra shook her head. "No, Princess," she replied. But I purposely visit the guard quarters regularly with extra supplies from the kitchen. I have asked around. I mentioned his name. No one will say anything." Although they were alone, Pietra dropped her voice to a whisper. "If your Savio is here, search the dungeon."

"Once little Rodrigo is settled, I shall go there," Lucrezia said.

The women continued to the waiting carriage, flanked by two soldiers. Rodrigo deployed the Vatican guard to retrieve the child from Vannozza's grip, and Lucrezia was sure it would be a long time before her mother gave forgiveness for taking her grandson away from her.

The driver helped a young woman from Vannozza's household from the carriage, who promptly placed Rodrigo in Lucrezia's anxious arms. She kissed the babe's tiny head and silently promised to find his father. The babe's little hand curled around her smallest finger. If only he knew how much he held her heart in his tiny palm.

She passed him to Pietra and said, "Bring him directly to my apartments. Post a guard outside. Allow no one entrance until I return."

Lucrezia knew the winding labyrinth to the palace dungeon, another place Burchard intentionally showed her. Strange how the macabre tour was the beginning of her royal captivity. Escaping the nunnery and keeping little Rodrigo was a triumph over her father she had never foreseen. A victory she would be foolish to rest on.

The long-ago excursion with Burchard had ended at the dungeon entrance. Constructed in his early days as Pope, her father built the cavernous prison chambers over the palace waste system, away from the royal finery. The filth eventually tunneled to the waters of the Tiber. Burchard had wrinkled his nose and pulled her away from the putrid stench wafting from the arched wooden door, warning her, "Stay away from this place. There is only suffering and death here."

Lucrezia approached the Vatican guards safeguarding the entrance. Damp, moss-covered walls shimmered from torches set into the rough stones. Lucrezia's breath was a warm mist against the cold dungeon air.

"Open the door," Lucrezia commanded the guards, her voice forceful.

The guards traded uneasy glances. Royal visits to the catacomb were rare, but to see the Pope's daughter standing before them was unheard of. Bound to duty, no matter how strange the circumstances, the smaller man opened the door and bowed while the brawnier sentry followed Lucrezia as she entered the dungeon.

"Allow me to escort you, Princess," the guard requested. "The prisoners can be unruly."

"Very well," Lucrezia replied, not wanting to argue and draw more unwanted attention.

They proceeded down a winding staircase. Wails and howls grew louder. The stench of human misery made her stomach turn, but the thought of Savio in such a vile place made her want to vomit.

At the bottom of the stairwell, an antechamber lined with cells faced each other. The sound of chaos resounded in Lucrezia's ears. Moans of the tortured mingled with the clang of metal. The relentless crack of a bullwhip sliced the air. To her left was a vast black bellow that kept the tips of assorted pokers glowing a fiery red. On her right, an older guard with a stooped back and milky blue eyes held up a hand to stop them.

Lucrezia wasted no time. "I am looking for the soldier, Savio Vitelli. You will show me where he is."

The man stroked his gray beard and gazed into Lucrezia's stern eyes. For a tense moment, Lucrezia feared they would refuse her demand, perhaps even scoff at her, but she stared back at the old gatekeeper without blinking.

"Princess, I will fulfill your request," he finally said. "The man you are looking for was brought in as a traitor two weeks ago on the Prefect's orders. He is considered a deserter. However, I must warn you that the inquisitor has been tough on him." As he spoke, he watched her closely for any sign of comprehension. Despite this news, she remained composed, knowing her beloved Savio was finally within reach.

"You will not be accountable," she replied, shaking with anger. She blamed Juan and no one else. Only he would answer for the atrocities her lover suffered at the hands of the inquisitor.

The old guard led her past the first few cells. Bare arms, covered in sores and filth, flailed out for mercy, and the soldier accompanying her knocked them away with the butt of his sheathed sword. Lucrezia shuddered at their touch.

They stopped in front of a cell, deathly quiet and dark. The guard reached for a torch, and the stooped man fumbled with a key to unlock the iron cage.

The dim entrance brightened when the guard settled the torch into a sconce inside the cell. At first, Lucrezia thought the cage was empty, but then her eyes adjusted. Hay was scattered on the cell floor, matted with urine and filth. A stool lay on its side. Savio lay curled in the corner. His flesh was torn from the whip. Bloody slashes ran the length of his torso, back, and legs. She rushed to him, sinking onto the hay, and cradled his bleeding head in her lap.

"Water!" she screamed at the stooped man, who hurried away and returned with a sloshing bucket of water.

Her scream roused Savio. "You are here," he said, opening his eyes, his voice brittle and parched.

Lucrezia offered him water, and Savio emptied the ladle in a desperate swallow, spilling more than he drank. Welts and bruises covered his face, but his bloodied hands made her recoil.

"Your father's inquisitor is talented." He grimaced, laid back on her lap, and curled his hands into fists to hide his missing fingernails. "Juan arrested me under the false guise of a traitor, but it is my love for you they need me to recant. Your family wants me to confess to rape. That I took you by force."

Hate for Juan pulsed within her, the remembrance of what he did to Pietra forever emblazoned in her memory. Her brother was the rapist, a repulsive degenerate.

"My love, do not utter such a vulgar lie. She turned to the old guard. "Release him immediately!"

The man shook his head. "Not without General Borgia or the Holy Father's consent. I am sorry, Princess."

Lucrezia ignored him and turned back to Savio. "You have a son," she told him, pressing her face to his. She would have given her life for a glimpse of happiness in his tired eyes.

"A boy?" he whispered. His lips curled into a weak smile.

"Yes, and he is handsome and strong like his father. We escaped the nunnery. He is here. You will see him. I promise. I will get you away from this place."

The sudden joy faded, and he looked away. "Do not promise me that. The danger is too great. Your father. Your brother. They will never let me rest. They will never allow us to be together. But, if this is my fate, we must let it be. Say our goodbyes while we still can."

"Don't say that," Lucrezia said. His words crushed her like a wall coming down, and her heart heaved with pain, but she could not ignore the truth in them. She kissed his cracked lips and caressed his cheek. "I will return."

She turned to the old man. "If the inquisitor comes near this man, kill him."

***

Lucrezia returned from the dungeon as fast as she could, wondering if she had the power to wield such a command at the old guard. Her dress was soiled, and her face was smeared with mud and tears. The palace's bright light and vivid colors hurt her eyes as she searched for Giulia.

She found her father's mistress playing with baby Laura in her bedchamber.

"Where is Rodrigo?" Lucrezia cried, barging in without knocking.

Giulia placed Laura in her cradle. "What has happened?" she asked, alarmed by Lucrezia's appearance.

"Tell me where my father is!" Lucrezia demanded again.

"Your father is gone," Giulia answered. "He left for Antium to view the progress of the new cathedral. He will return in two days."

"Too late... too late," Lucrezia repeated, feeling her legs weaken.

Giulia took Lucrezia by the shoulders and gave her a firm shake. "Calm yourself! Too late for what?"

"My Savio languishes in the Vatican dungeon only to be set free with my father's consent! Juan arrested him. Tortured him!" Lucrezia covered her face and sobbed.

Giulia gently pulled Lucrezia's hands from her tear-stained face. "A messenger arrived this morning. They hanged Girolamo Savonarola. The heretic. Your brother's mission is finished. He is due back from Florence this evening."

Juan's success was no surprise. She was sure the monk's death would surely please her father. But Juan's arrival had more to do with his captive in the dungeon than the conclusion of the uprising in Florence. Of that, she was certain.

***

Dinner with Cesare went on as planned. Lucrezia joined him in his private den. A modest meal of roasted meats, vegetables, and bread filled the table. He had begun the meal without her. His eyes glowed from the wine already consumed.

Lucrezia wasted no time telling her brother of her sorrowful plight and begging for his help.

Cesare waved her away. "I cannot help you. Not this time."

Lucrezia sat in shocked silence. The brother who promised to protect her, even kill for her, now refused.

"How can you not stand with me? Your sister!" she cried. "You are cruel and unworthy to call yourself my brother."

Her words were meant to harm, but Cesare picked up his wine goblet, gave it a swirl, and drank heartily. He told her, "Our father and brother are cruel. Place the blame where it belongs. What can I do? Rush the dungeon guards? Rescue your lover? To what end? So Father and Juan can retake him? Torture him some more, or worse?" The last two words dangled between them like the Dominican monk Juan hanged. "No, Sister, your battle is not with me. Now eat and drink with me," he said, finished with the subject. He waved a servant over to fill her goblet and offer a meat platter.

Lucrezia accepted the drink but not the food. She had no appetite except for the wine that numbed her head but not her heart.

"Father advised me of your plan to pass your child off as my own. You should have discussed it with me first, Sister," Cesare said, sinking his teeth into a thick piece of venison.

Lucrezia raised an eyebrow. "You will not agree?"

"I am agreeable to it," he replied, his mouth full of meat as he spoke. "The arrangement will not hinder my existence, but I resent not being asked beforehand. I do not care for surprises."

Lucrezia knew when to humble herself, even with Cesare. "Thank you, Brother. I apologize for not presenting the prospect to you first. However, I am grateful you are keen on the idea."

Cesare nodded, satisfied with her answer.

They dined mostly in silence. Lucrezia moved food around on her plate but accepted wine from the servant when her goblet was empty. As she sat in the company of her older brother, she pondered his delicate situation. Loathing the Cardinal red cape, the only chance for him to escape his religious station was to keep their father appeased. Do his bidding, even if it required Cesare to remain within the walls of the Vatican. There was talk of assembling bans of mercenaries. Small armies dispatched at the Pope's pleasure to keep the papal states in order. Stave off uprisings such as Florence. Perhaps Cesare hoped to lead such a covert band of soldiers. Lucrezia sighed. There was no shortage of Borgia battles to be fought. It only benefited her to understand Cesare's desire and dilemma.

Cesare reached for a piece of wild boar. His knife paused in midair, and his eyes gazed past Lucrezia. "Brother?"

Juan stood in the doorway, leaning against the wooden frame. His grin suggested he had been there all along. "A feast!" he declared and glanced around the room, taking in the meal and its occupants. "It has been long since I have supped with my brother and dear sister."

Her brother swaggered into the room, still donning his sword and traveling clothes. He nodded to Cesare, turned to Lucrezia, spread his arms, and said, "What? No greeting? Are you not happy to see me, Sister?"

Lucrezia shuddered. Sarcasm dripped from each word, and his sardonic smirk enraged her. Juan strutted to the table, pulled out a chair next to Lucrezia, and sat, not waiting for a servant. He stank of horse and sweat, and his eyes gleamed of wine. The candle flame gave them an unnatural glow.

Suddenly, Juan's demeanor changed. He scowled at Lucrezia as if his entrance had not elicited his desired response. "Is there something you mean to say?" he growled.

"Release Savio," she hissed, grateful that Cesare was present. He may not have agreed to aid her, but he would not let Juan harm her. Of that, she was sure.

"The traitor in the palace prison?" he replied, stabbing a pork loin from the platter. "Why would I do that?"

"He is innocent. You know I went to him willingly."

Juan brought the knife point down violently into the meat, making Lucrezia jump. "You think this a game? It is not! The house of Borgia sways in the balance!" He pointed at Cesare. "You are too busy fleeing the Cardinalship." He turned his finger at Lucrezia. "You are too eager spreading your legs for the Vatican army."

"Easy, Brother," Cesare warned.

Juan rose from his chair and paced the room, his agitation apparent. "Father has sacrificed much to move our dynasty forward," he continued. "Am I the only one who understands this? Florence is only the first of the papal states to undermine Father. They balk at fiefdoms and land gifted to clerics and allies and threaten to side with the French if Charles invades Naples, maybe even Milan. You are both self-serving children." He stared at Lucrezia. "Renew your allegiance to our father."

"My allegiance is to Savio, my son's father! The man tortured beneath this very room. The flesh torn from his body. Nails ripped from his fingers."

"Your allegiance is misplaced, Sister."

"Release him."

"I cannot. Leaving the nunnery with the child was a mistake. Now our family wastes time undoing what you've done." He emptied his goblet and poured another. Savio will recant or die."

Tears welled in Lucrezia's eyes, but she refused to let them fall.

Juan circled behind her chair and placed his hands on Lucrezia's shoulders. "How is the bastard son of yours? Does he sleep well?" He leaned in and whispered in her ear. "Has he taken fondly to your breast?"

Lucrezia shrugged him away, disgusted. "You will never know. I forbid you to see him."

"Really. Won't it be interesting when it comes time to baptize the child? Isn't that right, Cesare? Would it not be unusual for a brother not to attend? As the boy's father, I hope you have more say in his upbringing."

Cesare said nothing.

Juan put his hands on her again, but this time around her neck. His long fingers tightened on her throat, and the veins of her neck pulsed against his grip.

Cesare suddenly leaped forward and shoved him away. Juan stumbled backward but regained balance quickly, his eyes wild with anger. He swung madly at his brother, but Cesare dodged the haphazard blows, making Juan appear like an ill-tempered child pitching a fit.

Finally, Juan stopped. His chest heaved from exertion. He glared at his brother and sister. "Hear my words. Heed my warning. Abandon your ambition and expunge love from your heart. Father holds all our futures. We are the House of Borgia."

CHAPTER TWELVE

"Come with me." Cesare stood next to her bed. He had changed from his red Cardinal robe into everyday clothes, a riding cape, and black leather boots. His face was dark and severe. Pietra stood nervously behind him.

"I cannot go riding with you," Lucrezia said, rubbing the sleep from her eyes. After hours of pacing the floor the night before, Pietra finally convinced her to take an herbal elixir to help her sleep. "Drink this," her servant had said. "Sleep. You will need all your strength tomorrow to battle with your father."

Lucrezia had spent most of that evening devising a plan to present to her father. Any hope of saving Savio rested on him. The odds of her father letting them be together were remote. That truth had settled in her bones and hardened in her heart. But he could let Savio live if he wanted. Banish him forever from entering Vatican City. Then, perhaps someday, she would find him again.

"Come with me," Cesare said again, this time more forcefully.

"I must go to Father."

"You will come with me. Get dressed."

***

All four men hung from a stone bridge close to the palace: Savio, the stooped guard with milky eyes, the soldier who escorted her, even the guard who had opened the prison door. Hands and ankles were bound with rope; the cool morning breeze swayed the lifeless bodies like gruesome, silent wind chimes.

She did not know she was screaming until Cesare's palm struck her cheek. Then there was darkness, and she was dreaming. Rodrigo was no longer a baby but a small boy. Savio chased him on a winding garden path, lush and beautiful. Laughter lingered in the air like a summer song. Rodrigo held a ball in his tiny hands and threw it to Savio, who tossed it back with a loving smile. The dream dimmed, then became clear again. Now Lucrezia was being chased, but the game had changed. The air had cooled. A dark forest replaced the garden. She ran the way she did as a little girl, those days long ago when her father playfully chased her. Rodrigo's voice called for her to stop, and she did. He held something in his hands, perhaps a ball. She could not be sure. He threw it to her, and what she caught was not a ball but a bleeding heart, still beating. Savio's heart was bleeding in her hands. This time, she heard herself scream, and she awakened.

Pietra stood at the foot of her bed. "Your baby cries for you."

Lucrezia turned away and pulled the coverlet tightly around her. "Has he not been with the wet nurse?"

She barely remembered Cesare bringing her back to the palace, limp and in shock. Pietra explained how Cesare secretly made his way to her bedchamber so as not to cause a scene. Now, finally awake, life rang hollow. Yet, much to her dismay, her existence continued beyond her control, a drama with her as an unwilling participant.

"He is with the wet nurse now, Princess, but no one can replace a mother's touch. May I bring him to you?"

"No."

"Some food then?"

"No."

"You worry me," the girl said and tossed another log in the fireplace.

Pietra was right to be concerned, Lucrezia thought. The vision of Savio hanging from the bridge left her languishing in bed for days, refusing to see anyone. Even the thought of her crying baby did not rouse her. She had failed to save her one true love. Life was useless, a pointless charade. She knew happiness would never be hers in this lifetime, perhaps not even in the next.

Even her father came to her, the one person she could not refuse, claiming not to know of Juan's plan to execute Savio, as if the denial would comfort her. "Your brother was wrong to proceed without my knowledge," he had told her, sounding as if the situation was merely unfortunate.

"Would the outcome have been any different, Father, had you known?" she cried.

"What is done is done," he replied before leaving, his voice cold and indifferent.

The following morning, Pietra entered carrying a tray of warm mead, bread, and cheese. She purposefully placed it on the small table close to Lucrezia. The fragrant mead and fresh bread pained her empty stomach.

"Your father has ordered your presence at a banquet feast this evening," Pietra told her.

"I am unwell," Lucrezia replied and buried her head into her silk pillow.

"He insists," Pietra replied. "Adriana told me herself. Your father has betrothed Juan to Maria Enriquez de Luna. He is to become Duke of Gandia. The feast is in his honor."

The word "honor" pricked at Lucrezia's heart. To speak of honor and her brother in the same breath was profane. Her grief shifted to anger, a rage that inflamed her inside and out.

"It upsets you, I know," Pietra said. It upsets me, too. Juan is unhappy with the match your father made for him." Pietra's voice softened. Her eyes filled with tears. "Your brother still comes to me. He takes me by force. I am afraid once he leaves the palace to become duke, he will take me away, too. Take me away from you."

Lucrezia pushed back the coverlet and sat up.

Pietra used the opportunity to sit next to Lucrezia. She held out her hand and opened a calloused palm. She held a familiar tiny flask. "Cantarella," Pietra said. "I still have it."

Lucrezia remembered the story of Pietra's father and his swift yet painful death. She reached for the cup of mead and warm bread. "Tonight," Lucrezia said. "I must do it tonight. Draw me a bath. Have Adriana find me a gown. Make sure it is of the deepest black," she paused while she chewed and swallowed a mouthful of sweet bread, then added, "and have the wet nurse bring me my son."

***

Adriana did not disappoint her. The gown was of the deepest black, like a night without the moon or stars, with elegant gray velvet trim. The plain silk pleats created stunning folds from Lucrezia's waist to the floor. The bodice was adorned with black onyx stones arranged in a chevron pattern, leading up to a ruffled neckline. Lucrezia's braided hair was held in place by a black netted trinzale laced with black pearls.

Her father and brothers had already taken their places at the high table, flanked by two lower tables opposite one another with a dance floor in the center. Her tardiness was intentional. A meal of fine meats and royal delicacies graced the table. The servants had already begun offering guests choice pieces of game, puddings, and pickled vegetables.

A hushed silence fell upon the hall as Lucrezia entered the room and slowly climbed the few steps to take her seat between her brothers. Her measured gait was deliberate, a dramatic show for the crowded room. A frown crossed Rodrigo's lips, and his eyes swept over her with a wave of anger she could feel. His stern eyes circled the room, and the banqueters resumed their amiable chatter. From under the table, Cesare embraced her hand with a slight squeeze.

"You wear the color of mourning to my betrothal feast?" Juan seethed in her ear. "You dare flaunt your dead lover even now?"

Lucrezia stoically stared at the surrounding merriment, undeterred by her brother's anger. "I am told this betrothal is joyless. Perhaps I mourn your impending unhappiness," she answered with sarcasm.

Maria Enriquez was the niece of King Ferdinand of Aragon and Queen Isabella. In keeping with a longtime alliance with Spain, Rodrigo sought to strengthen the ties with this important ally, especially since Spain was keen on defending Italy from France. Rumors persisted that Maria was intelligent and devout but not too pleasing to the eye. A large portrait of the girl was displayed on a wooden tripod, the focal point of the banquet in the center of the dance floor.

Maria was still in Spain. It was customary to commission artists to capture the likeness of faraway brides-to-be. Ambassadors delivered the portraits to future husbands for approval. The artist had done his best with the subject he had to work with. Maria sat in an orchard on a garden bench in full form, not the usual up-close depiction. The purple hues of her royal gown did little to improve her washed-out complexion, and the gabled headdress hid her hair, exposing an unnaturally high hairline and broad forehead. Her vacant eyes looked forlornly somewhere in the distance as she held a bouquet of orange blossoms, a symbol of happiness and fertility.

Lucrezia cocked her head at the painting. "Your bride looks as frightened as a little bird, a tiny starling afraid to take flight."

Juan motioned for a servant to fill his goblet. "My little bird from across the sea has nothing to fear," he replied, swirling the wine before downing the entire glass. "I shall bed her long enough to produce an heir, perhaps a few more for good measure." He called for the servant again and pointed to his empty glass. "Now, *your* little bird is quite a different matter," he replied. "Little Pietra keeps me quite satisfied. She must have mentioned it. I enjoy her so much, and she will be a fine addition to my new household."

Lucrezia stiffened. "Have you not taken enough from me?"

"Not nearly enough," Juan answered matter-of-factly. "Especially considering your theatrics this evening."

"You cannot have her," Lucrezia said.

"I can, and I will." The tenor rose in his voice, catching Rodrigo's attention. "I shall take her tonight! Now that my engagement is official, I need not wait for a wife to create my household."

Rodrigo gritted his teeth. "You behave as commoners," he seethed at Lucrezia and Juan. "Do not forget your place!"

Juan leaned uncomfortably close to Lucrezia. "Have her ready. I take her tonight."

A good while after the banquet, Juan staggered into Lucrezia's bedchamber, drunk on mead. He sat down opposite his sister. Lucrezia's eyes were red and swollen from crying.

"Tears will not save your servant," Juan smirked.

"Pietra's leaving no longer upsets me," Lucrezia said, brushing a tear from her cheek.

"No? Then why do you weep like a child?"

"I was mistaken, Brother. Pietra is not the loyal servant I thought she was. Adriana came to me. She found this hidden under the girl's featherbed." Lucrezia pointed to five onyx stones on the table resting in a shallow bowl. "She must have taken them from my gown while putting it away. She is a thief. My heart breaks once more."

"You give your heart away too easily, Sister, which is why taking what pleases you is better than giving love away."

Pietra stood dutifully next to Juan's chair. Head bowed in disgrace at the allegation. Juan planted a hard swat on the girl's backside. Pietra flinched but did not cry out.

"Like a dog, I will teach her to heel," Juan said. "She will not steal from me. I will take her hand off with my sword if she tries." He swatted her again. "Bring us some wine!"

Pietra disappeared.

Flames from the fireplace cast a yellow, sickly hue on Juan's pocked face. Age had settled hard on her brother with his countless years of whoring and drink. He appeared far older than his twenty years.

She remembered him as a small boy. With his mischievous ways and quick wit, he was the favored son, even then. Cesare and Juan loved to challenge each other. Lucrezia often found the twosome daring who would let go of the tallest tree branch first or who dared to swim the widest, swiftest bend of a river.

Juan conquered Cesare at almost all their silly contests back then, but one unlucky day crossed Lucrezia's mind. The two brothers decided to race their little ponies, challenging whose miniature steed would soar over the stonewall first. Juan's saddle slipped to one side mid-air, and his arm twisted and broke. Lucrezia visited him that evening in his bedchamber after the surgeon had set the bone.

"I held my tongue, Sister," Juan proudly told her with slurred words. His arm rested on a pillow, bandaged from the shoulder to the forearm. "That nasty man pulled and tugged my arm into place. It snapped. I heard it," he mumbled, "but I laid here, still." His eyes drooped from the laudanum, and his voice drifted between awareness and sleep.

She brushed his young cheek with her palm to soothe him and noticed a welt under his eye. "Juan," she had whispered, "why is your eye bruised? Did you injure it, too, in the fall?"

He rolled over suddenly as if remembering a dreadful moment and yelled as his bandaged arm fell from the pillow. "Father," he whispered hoarsely. "It was Father. He said I must learn a lesson."

"What lesson?" Lucrezia asked, shocked at the time that her father was capable of such cruelty.

"Borgias don't fall... Borgias don't fail..." he murmured and drifted into unconsciousness. Lucrezia gently lifted the injured arm and laid it back on the cushion. His face became tranquil, and it brought Lucrezia peace.

Only later did Cesare admit to her that he loosened the saddle girth to cause the accident.

"Why do such a thing?" she had asked. "Father beat him because of the fall!"

Cesare shrugged and brushed his pony's russet mane. "Nevertheless, it is an excellent lesson learned. Juan cannot always win."

"You cheated!" she said, amazed at his indifference. "I shall tell Father, and then it will be you with a bruised eye."

He shrugged again. "Father will see it as part of the lesson. Trust me, dear Sister. Our father has also given me my fair share of lessons."

The conversation ended there, and so did the remembrance of little Juan's broken arm and the bruise left by Rodrigo. That day was never discussed again. But the memory stuck with her. Why had it resurfaced now? She did not know. She knew that Juan's abuse was no excuse for the pain he inflicted on others, the violence that somehow soothed his wounded, pathetic soul.

"He called for you," Juan suddenly said, returning her to the moment. "Your man called your name repeatedly as they placed the noose around his neck. I thought you should know. Quite touching." His voice remained neutral as if it had not moved him at all in truth.

"Stop," Lucrezia whispered. Was there no end to his cruelty?

"Alas, his neck did not break on impact like that heretic Girolamo's. Instead, your man writhed like a trout caught on a fishing line, thrashing about before he finally went limp."

Lucrezia felt her heartbeat thumping in her chest. She heard it in her head- a brash rhythm, pounding out a tempo of revenge. Pietra appeared with a wine vessel and two goblets already filled. She set the tray on the side table with an awkward thud. Her hands shook, and beads of sweat covered her top lip. Juan was sure to notice, too, she thought. She wanted to warn Pietra to take care, but Juan beat her to it.

"Careful!" Juan scolded. His eyes darted to the goblets, then back to Pietra. "Bring it to me, clumsy cow, before you spill it!"

Pietra peered at Lucrezia, who cocked her head slightly and gave the girl the smallest of nods.

Her faithful servant handed them both a glass, bowed, and backed away, knowing what was to ensue.

Lucrezia did not partake but observed her brother down the toxic liquid in three hearty swallows.

Lucrezia waited.

Juan belched, then told her, "Now that the nasty business of your lover is behind us, I am sure Father will waste no time finding you another match." His fingers lightly stroked his beard.

Lucrezia watched.

"Father tells me your bastard child is to remain here," Juan continued, staring at the bottom of his empty glass. "Not a decision I agree with." Suddenly, his eyes widened with unexpected panic. He lurched forward in his chair and crumbled onto the carpet.

Lucrezia moved to Pietra and gripped her hand. They stood silent and paralyzed at the sight of Juan shaking violently on the floor. The cantarella's effects happened quickly, just as Pietra had described with her father's death.

Bile and foam spewed from Juan's mouth and down his cheeks. He clawed at his neck; his throat clasped tight in a painful spasm. The whites of his eyes turned scarlet as tears of blood oozed and bubbled. His bloodied eyes locked on hers. She could not look away. Juan shook violently, then abruptly stopped, but his eyes remained open, a twisted grimace forever etched on his face.

"It is over," Pietra whispered.

"Not yet. We must get rid of him," Lucrezia answered, breaking away from her brother's deadly gaze. "I have a plan. We'll drag him to my privy and dump him down the cesspit. He will go through the waste tunnels and eventually empty into the Tiber."

Petra frowned. "You believe this will work?" she asked fretfully.

"We have no choice. Besides, the river is teeming with other unfortunate, misbegotten souls."

"If it is the only way, it must be done." Pietra agreed. "But first...," she pulled a dagger from her apron pocket.

"What are you doing? Are you mad? He is dead!"

Ignoring her mistress, the girl sank to her knees and plunged the dagger into Juan's torso repeatedly. Her blows became frantic and violent, a rage finally set free.

Lucrezia did not stop her, and eventually, Pietra slumped back on her haunches, panting. Specks of blood dotted her face. Her white linen apron was now red.

"No one can suspect death by poison," Pietra said, wiping her mouth with the back of her hand. "Cantarella is as common among the rich as it is poor. So, what caused his death must not be a mystery. Anyone will see he was stabbed to death, not poisoned."

Lucrezia was thankful for Pietra's insight. Of course, royalty administered poison to their enemies as regularly as peasants, but a violent stabbing would make bandits or jealous lovers more believable.

"Let's get on with it," Lucrezia said, folding both sides of the carpet over the corpse.

Pietra nodded in agreement, and they both stooped and took hold of the Persian fabric, Lucrezia at the head and Pietra at the feet. The body was heavy and clumsy to carry. Nevertheless, they half-carried and half-dragged the corpse to Lucrezia's privy room and shut the door.

Lucrezia's privy was the smallest in her apostolic apartment, meant only for her and a chambermaid, who assisted during her daily regimen. Besides the marble privy stall, only a matching stand with a porcelain wash basin stood in the corner.

Lucrezia opened the privy seat, revealing the vast darkness beneath. "Feet first," Lucrezia said, sizing up the wide cesspit hole. "Remove his boots and the waist belt. Make haste!"

Pietra did as she asked, and together, they raised the corpse and slipped Juan's legs down the privy. The rest of his body followed with a long silence before the sickening splash as he entered the foul cesspit far beneath the palace. Lucrezia flung Juan's boots and waist belt after him, and they, too, made a nauseating, watery thud. Pietra untied her bloodied apron and tossed it down the hole.

Lucrezia grasped Pietra's hand. "He will torture us no more."

"Wait," Pietra said and hurried away. She rushed back with the decanter of poisoned wine and the two glasses, tossed them down the hole, and then looked at her mistress. "Now it is finished."

CHAPTER THIRTEEN

"No sign of him, Your Holiness." The Vatican guard knelt at Rodrigo's feet with a long sword at his side and a plumed helmet in hand.

Juan's disappearance had lasted three days. Rodrigo organized a search party to find him. Her father had gathered his remaining family in his private den to await news, except for Cesare, who insisted on joining the search for his brother. Lucrezia busied herself with needlework and gently rocked little Rodrigo's cradle with her slippered foot.

"See that you check all the whorehouses, all the taverns, gaming halls, and hostelries. Turn Rome upside down! Find my son!"

"Yes, Your Holiness." The soldier kissed her father's signet ring and disappeared.

Giulia sat next to Rodrigo on the settee, holding baby Laura. Lucrezia knew it annoyed Giulia when she was not at the center of her father's world, even if the distraction was the man's missing son. "All will be well, my love," she said with large, concerned eyes, stroking Rodrigo's hand.

He snatched his hand away, not wishing to be consoled. Dark circles hung beneath his bloodshot eyes. "Juan has never been absent this long. Not without knowing his whereabouts. Something is amiss. I feel it in my bones. If they find him drunken in a whorehouse, he will pay the price! I swear to God Almighty Himself!"

No, Lucrezia thought, pulling the silver thread tight. Except for a blackened eye for failing to jump a stonewall as a boy, her father had never held Juan accountable for anything. Until now, it was by her hand that he had answered for his many sins, not the power of the Pope or God himself. She did the deed that many held secret in their heart, royals and commoners alike. Juan may have been the son of a Pope, but he had gained no friends. His enemies were many; even if they bowed to Juan and bent their knee to the Borgia regime, Juan was hated.

Rodrigo's gaze settled on Lucrezia. "You quarreled with your brother at his engagement party. Enraged him with your black mourning gown," he said pointedly. "What are your thoughts on Juan's whereabouts? Your brother, who you hold so *dear* to your heart."

Lucrezia willed her hand to remain steady with the needle as her heart fluttered like a frightened hare. "Juan came to my apartments after the banquet. He was angry - as was I. We sorted the matter out, Father, the best we could. Juan will never receive my forgiveness, but we are Borgias. As you once told me, what is done is done." She winced as the needle slipped and pricked her finger. A drop of deep red blood seeped into the bright white fabric.

Rodrigo grunted, and his eyes narrowed as he pondered her answer carefully.

The mantle clock struck three bells at midday, and the wait was over. Cesare entered Rodrigo's apartment, ragged and drawn. He went to their father, still perched on the settee, and grasped Rodrigo's hands. "We have found Juan, Father," Cesare said, his voice straining.

Rodrigo's face twisted with confusion. "Where is he? Bring him here immediately!"

Cesare's head dipped as if the words were too heavy to speak. "We found him in the Tiber, Father. Stabbed and drowned."

Rodrigo's face froze in disbelief. "It cannot be! You speak lies!" He shoved Cesare away.

"It is true, Father. I brought him to your private chapel. He lies there in repose."

Rodrigo rushed from the room. Giulia was not far behind.

Lucrezia tossed aside her soiled needlework and approached her brother. "It is true? Juan is dead?" Her voice was calm and composed.

"Juan is dead," Cesare repeated.

She took a step back, distancing herself from his words. "How was he found?" she asked.

"We traveled the riverbank down to the central district, thinking he may have visited the Jewish ghetto. We questioned people as we went. Finally, a friar peddling relics told us of a masked man on horseback. He said this man carried a slumped body over a saddle and dumped it in the river late last night. The friar wondered if this could be the man we sought."

Lucrezia's heart raced. Dominic? Could it be? She wanted to ask about the monk's hair color. Was he young or old? Did he travel with a woman? Lucrezia forced the thought from her mind. Hundreds of religious people flocked to the central district, eager to sell their holy wares to the desperate seeking redemption. Instead, she said, "This friar did not intervene?"

"Dumping dead bodies into the Tiber is not unusual, Sister. The man wished he had a ducat for every forsaken soul he saw end up in the river. Boatmen scoured the river bottom. A fisherman found our brother several hours later."

"Do you think bandits ambushed Juan?"

"Perhaps. Someone ran a dagger through his torso many times," Cesare rubbed his forehead, "and his boots were missing, but his ducat purse remained attached to his doublet."

Lucrezia stiffened. In their haste, she and Pietra had forgotten to dispose of Juan's purse.

Cesare circled the room like a confined animal. "What marauding bandit forgets a pouch brimming with ducats?" he asked.

"Perhaps the bandit panicked. Knew the friar was watching him," Lucrezia offered, trying to remain calm.

Cesare scowled. "Perhaps."

The weight of his eyes held her captive.

"I am as perplexed as you, Brother," Lucrezia said, turning her back to escape his gaze.

As fast as the words left her lips, Cesare was just as quick. He lunged, twisting her around, his hands tight on her arms. "You lie, Sister!" he cried, his face washed in pain and anger. "You think me a fool? Me? Your Cesare? You were the last to see our brother! You sought revenge for your dead lover with your gown of black. You and Juan argued. Then, he inexplicably vanished! I know the depths of your grief, Sister! I carried your stricken body in my arms." He pulled her face uncomfortably close to his. "Your heart untethered from your beloved too easily," he seethed. "You resolved the conflict with our brother too fast! Your story about making amends is a lie!"

"Unhand me!" she cried and, despite his strength, tore away from his grip. "Ask me, Brother, what you wish. Be direct, and I will provide an honest answer, but do not think for an instant that I will tolerate brutality from you or anyone."

A heavy knock sounded on the door. Lucrezia hurried to oblige entry, not caring who it was, only grateful for the interruption. Burchard greeted her with a curious frown. Under his arm, he carried several scrolls. He stepped into the room and peeked around.

"I was on my way to the apostolic library," her father's secretary said. Loud voices drew my attention. Is all well here?" His solemn eyes glanced at Cesare and then back at Lucrezia.

"Quite," Lucrezia answered. She steeled herself against Burchard's stern observation.

"Not exactly," Cesare said, curling his arm around Lucrezia's shoulders in an awkward embrace, his voice returning to a casual yet strained tone. "My sister and I are distraught over the death of our brother and wish to grieve alone."

"Murder," Burchard corrected.

Cesare cocked his head, confused.

"You mean Juan's murder. Your brother was stabbed repeatedly, then drowned," Burchard said, tapping the tightly rolled papers under his arm. "The tragic report is here, ready to be installed forever in the Vatican archives."

"Of course," Cesare replied, "murder."

"We appreciate your concern," Lucrezia said. She moved back to the door and motioned for Burchard to take his leave. "As a servant, you always have the well-being of the Borgia family at heart. Your loyalty is unwavering and truly appreciated, particularly during this time of suffering."

Ignoring Lucrezia's hollow praise, Burchard sniffed at the word "servant" and brusquely left the room.

Cesare sunk into the chaise near the fireplace and stared into the crackling flames. Lucrezia sat down gently beside him.

"Ask," she said.

After a long pause, Cesare said, "Did you kill him? Our brother?"

"Yes," Lucrezia said.

Cesare paused again. "With your own hands?"

"Yes," she said again.

"No one aided you."

"No," she lied, then covered Cesare's hands with her own. The deceit was necessary to protect Pietra.

Cesare stared at her slim fingers, seeing them for the first time as an instrument of murder. "I see," he said.

"Many suffered at the whim of our 'cherished' brother, not just myself and Savio," she continued, desperate for him to understand what she had known for a long time. "Many wished him dead. That truth cannot be denied. Juan was not long for this world. He thought himself invincible, but he did inhuman acts. So I did what someone else would have eventually done to him." Lucrezia took a deep breath. "Put this ugliness behind us, Brother. Think of all you can accomplish with Juan gone. Father will need another warrior, a Borgia protector, a soldier to fight our battles and avenge his son's death," she added and squeezed his fingers. "Throw off your Cardinal robe. Be the man you have always wanted."

Cesare pulled his hands away from hers and stood. "You are right. It is what I want. I only wish it could have come about differently. I understand Juan was capable of horrific atrocities. I am sorry for the pain he caused you, but I never wished him dead. You know that." He held out his hand to her. "We must go to Father now. Share in his grief and lay Juan to rest."

"Very well," Lucrezia said and allowed Cesare to help her rise, not sure if she had failed to alter his heart or if his words were true, "but before we do, know this too, as far as my beloved Savio is concerned, I untether nothing."

***

Days passed before they announced Juan's burial. Rodrigo remained with his son's reposed body, wailing, demanding the cold, lifeless body to rise like Lazarus and walk the earth again. Be the Vatican Prefect and favored son again. Once the corpse left the palace to be cleaned and prepared, her father spent much of the time confined to bed, grief-stricken and inconsolable, until Giulia finally roused him.

Pietra straightened Lucrezia's black beaded headdress on the morning of Juan's Requiem Mass, the same one worn only weeks earlier at his betrothal banquet. Lucrezia noted the girl's calm presence as her steady hands made slight adjustments. She looked into Lucrezia's eyes with a contented smile as if a heavy stone had been lifted. The two did not speak of the dreadful secret they shared, and Lucrezia vowed to put it out of her mind forever the instant the funeral was over, burying the memory of Juan along with his body.

At midday, the mourning bells of the Basilica di Santa Maria rang through the streets of Rome's center. One hundred torchbearers led Juan's funeral procession into the domed baroque church built in honor of the Virgin Mary. The family followed the ornately carved litter at a slow, solemn gait as the eyes of the crowded congregation fell upon them. Laid out in his military uniform and absent of all ambition and cruelty, Juan's face was more peaceful in death than it had ever been in life.

Vannozza trailed slightly behind Rodrigo, with Guilia sulking even further behind. As predicted, Giulia's temper flared when told the Pope's former mistress was to be in the procession.

"They both lost the same child," Lucrezia told Giulia before her mother's arrival. "If you love Rodrigo, let it be. Allow them to share their grief."

As Lucrezia walked with Cesare at her side, a pang of guilt tugged at her heart for her mother's pain. She prayed fervently that the woman would never know the truth about her son's violent end. Black Milanese lace covered Vannozza's face, and she donned a flowing mourning gown. The news of Juan's death hit her hard. Perhaps because of all her children, he had been most like her, passionate and volatile but with a cruel heart. However, no grief compared to her father's sorrow. After Juan's interment in the Santa Maria catacomb, Rodrigo brazenly embraced Vannozza at the reception in the grand hall, openly weeping in her arms. Royals and religious exchanged anxious glances until, at Cesare's insistence, groomsmen led their father away to his apartment to rest.

Later, Lucrezia received her mother in her apartment. Vannozza reclined on a silk chaise near her daughter and slowly sipped warmed wine. Dark circles rimmed her eyes, still wet with grief. Exhaustion, if not sorrow, overwhelmed Lucrezia, too. She cuddled little Rodrigo and let him suckle her breast, relieved no harm would come to him, at least not at the hands of her brother. Vannozza watched Lucrezia longingly.

"Do you wish to hold him?" Lucrezia asked.

"I do," Vannozza replied, her voice barely a whisper, eyes again filled with tears.

"Of course." Lucrezia rose and placed the babe on Vannozza's lap.

"I shall leave on the morrow," she told Lucrezia. "The whore, Giulia, can console your father now. I will return to life on my farm. Mourn Juan on my own. My only prayer is that the murderer is found. Juan's death avenged."

"It is my prayer, as well." Lucrezia shifted uncomfortably. "Did Father mention a course of action for finding the murderer?" she asked, a pit of foreboding growing in her stomach.

"He has not."

"What if they never find this assailant, Mother?"

Vannozza stared at her grandson and caressed his cheek. "You forget your father is Pope Alexander Sextus of Rome. He will find the coward who murdered Juan. Anger has not yet overtaken his grief, but it will. I've seen Rodrigo's rage. The killer will be discovered. Nothing stays buried forever."

***

Rodrigo granted Cesare's request and released him from his Cardinal's vow shortly after Juan's burial. The Borgia dynasty shifted, and all felt the change. No longer was there a Borgia General Prefect to protect and handle Borgia interests. Yet, instead of placing Cesare in Juan's former position, Cesare commanded a band of renegade Vatican soldiers, an army of mercenaries, to do Rodrigo's bidding. Even as grief propelled her father into profound sadness, he held firm to his constant stratagem, plans to keep the Borgia strength firmly grounded within the walls of Vatican City and afar.

Cesare greeted Lucrezia in the south garden. Winter was upon Rome, but Lucrezia strolled the stone, manicured paths in need of solace and the fresh cold air she hoped would liven her spirit. Her brother sidled up next to her and gave her fur-draped shoulders a gentle squeeze. Finished with the Cardinal's red robe, Cesare wore a rich green doublet bordered with gold brocade and a woolen riding cape. He donned a matching velvet biretta on his head instead of the Cardinal's red zucchetto. In the slanted rays of the afternoon, he shimmered with the new power he now possessed.

"How is Father?" she asked, slipping her arm into the crook of his.

Cesare sighed. "Gripped with melancholy. I pray it subsides soon. There is a shift inside these Vatican walls. Our enemies see an opportunity to advance."

"Time is a swift current, and with it, all things change, as will his grief," Lucrezia said, caring little about her father's grief. Still, the mention of his foes piqued her interest. "What of these Borgia enemies? What do they hold against him?"

"Cardinals Orsini and Colonna spread the word of father's avarice and slowness to reform the church. Do you not remember his election promises?"

Lucrezia wanted to remind her brother that, at the time, she was but a child dreaming of her groom, Don Gaspare, and a wedding that never took place. "I do not," Lucrezia replied.

Cesare continued, "Our father gained his elevation through campaign pledges and vows to reform monasteries and churches. He promised to abolish unfair taxes collected from serfs who farmed the holy land. The feudal system was to be revised." Cesare breathed in deeply and exhaled, turning his face to the winter sun, the warmth seeping into his pores. "There is talk of Father leaving the city for a while. Embarking on a short crusade to heal his heart." Cesare chuckled softly, unable to help himself. "Our father tells his Cardinals his travels and fasting will reveal Juan's murderer. Bring him peace. This may be the plan he proclaims outwardly, but the man's schemes are bottomless. Who knows his true intentions."

"Ambition bested our father, I fear," Lucrezia said. Cesare's profile in the sun's reflection looked strikingly like her father's. "And what of you, dear Brother? What has our father devised for you?"

"I travel to France. Solidify our alliance with the new King Louis. Deliver to him his decree of divorce. The passing of Charles has left us a king to be molded to our liking, especially since Father has granted a solution to the discord with his wife. King Louis has already promised me the hand of Princess Charlotte d'Albret, sister of the King of Navarre. I shall be Duke of Valentinois and gain a hefty estate. Then, with the backing of France, I will defend Italy against our enemies. How is that, dear Sister, for a plan?" Cesare said, satisfied with his answer.

"What of my son?" she asked, her pulse quickened with dread. "You will take him away to France."

Cesare shook his head. "He will remain with you," Cesare replied. "I would not deny a child his earthly mother. He is supposed to be my child now, is he not? My duty is to do what is best for him."

"Father will not be pleased," she said as her heart swelled with the news.

"My happiness in France is more important than the future of a son who is not mine. Father would be unwise to send me away in a sour mood." His voice was confident with his position. Cesare was no stranger to gameplay with Rodrigo.

Lucrezia let her head rest against his shoulder. "Thank you, Cesare. This decision brings me more joy than you know, and I am also happy for you. Finally, you shall leave Vatican City, both a Borgia soldier and a nobleman—redeemed and renewed—the warrior you always dreamt of becoming."

"Your support is appreciated, Sister. I shall miss you."

Lucrezia paused for a moment, then asked, "What of love?"

"Love?"

"What if this Charlotte pleases you everywhere but your heart?"

"Then I will find someone else to please my heart," Cesare replied with a cavalier laugh.

Lucrezia marveled at the ease Cesare maneuvered the world around him. She swallowed the jealousy that swelled in her throat at his ability to toss away what displeased him and take what he wanted, pluck from life whatever joy he fancied.

Cesare stopped and turned to Lucrezia, having reached the path's end. "Go to Father. There will be plans for you to marry again. He is vulnerable now and can be swayed to give you a more joyful match."

She listened to her brother's advice with great attention. Cesare was clever in the ways of manipulation, and his words made her mind spin with attaining more than just an advantageous marriage but, perhaps, a means to a happier life. But thoughts of Savio surfaced. She missed how he looked at her, his eyes drinking in her whole being, his powerful arms that made her feel so safe. Tears pricked her eyes. Imagining herself with anyone else seemed impossible, but Cesare was right. Her father's grief benefited her. No marriage would replace the love she shared with Savio. Perhaps she could mitigate a union similar to Giovanni's, an amicable understanding.

Lucrezia grasped Cesare by his shoulders and hugged him tightly. They had never been apart for very long, and the thought of being without him frightened her. They had changed since their father became Pope Alexander VI, and not for the better. The winter wind swirled around them, cold and penetrating. She looked at him with a teary smile. "I shall miss you, Cesare."

CHAPTER FOURTEEN

Rodrigo's apartment chapel was more magnificent than any of the chapels in the palace. A large crucifix made from a single piece of olive wood hung over a marble altar. In a corner, there was a table with candles lit for the Pope's prayer intentions. The holy statue of Saint Peter, the foundation of the Catholic Church, looked down at the flames in contemplation. Lucrezia pondered how many candles were for Juan's sake, knowing none were lit for her.

Lucrezia discovered her father kneeling on the hard marble tile instead of the red velvet cushion before the altar. The air was filled with the scent of pungent and sweet frankincense. She found it strange that her father did not notice her as she entered the chapel, as his eyes were fixed on the crucifix above him. Gently, she placed her hand on his shoulder and said, "Father?"

He turned and looked at her with gray eyes as cold and vacant as the sea. His balding head was without its usual skull cap. Dressed in a simple white dressing gown, he appeared shriveled and depleted, his usual pomp and pageantry set aside. He blinked, and her presence came into focus.

"What is it, Daughter?"

Lucrezia motioned for him to rise. When he did, she took his damp hand like a parent would a child's and tenderly led him from the cold chamber into the warmth and comfort of his papal den. She pointed to a chair nearest the lit fireplace, and he sat.

Three days passed since Lucrezia's stroll with Cesare in the garden. Before approaching her father, she needed time to contemplate what she wished to accomplish. Now that the time had come, her promise to aid Lorena's search for her child was of paramount importance. Juan's death made Rodrigo vulnerable, exposed in a way Lucrezia hoped to influence and use to her advantage. Escaping the palace, if only briefly, was essential if her oath was to be kept.

"You worry me," Lucrezia stated simply.

"My son is gone," he answered, his eyes somewhere off in the distance.

"Cesare is here, as am I."

"Your brother is bound for France. He leaves in two days. His duty is there now. An alliance with France and a French marriage will keep our foreign enemies at bay."

"And what of you, Father?" she asked.

His eyes widened at the question. "I am Pope Alexander," he growled as if suddenly remembering.

"Grief overwhelms you, and rightly so, but you must not let those undermining your position view your mourning as vulnerability."

"They would be unwise to do so," Rodrigo grunted and turned his gaze on her with eyes less clouded. "We are House of Borgia. We must go on," he replied as if to remind himself.

"Cesare says you may embark on a pilgrimage. Heal your heart in the wake of Juan's death."

Her father's face twisted into a scowl. "I considered it," he conceded, sounding more like himself. "But, the papal states are in turmoil, and their impertinence must be addressed."

Lucrezia stood and reached for the silver decanter on the side table. "Whatever course you decide will be best," she answered diplomatically, pouring them a goblet of wine.

"We are no longer in favor with the Spanish," Rodrigo said, accepting the glass. "King Ferdinand and his mettlesome queen are displeased with our rekindled friendship with France, even after I declared the new world their territory. What do they know of the dark

politics and treachery on our very doorstep? Nothing!"
he spat. "Spain looks after Spain. They sit in the comfort
and safety of their thrones, casting nets across the sea to
further their domain. At the same time, I am charged with
God's Christendom throughout the world and protecting
the seat of Saint Peter." Rodrigo waved his hand at the
king and queen's irrelevance. "Romagna is in disarray,
divided, and at risk of being usurped by Venice, Milan, and
Florence. We must address their defiance."

"Would it not be prudent to send Cesare there instead of
France? Bring the Romagna barons under your obedience
and show these usurpers your power has not waned?"

Rodrigo's lip curled into a half-smile, the color
returning to his sallow cheeks. "Still the strategist, I see,"
he said and swallowed a hearty drink of wine. "Cesare
will return Romagna to the church's fold in due time.
But, of course, we can accomplish nothing without his
French marriage. Once we have that, Romagna will feel
our wrath." He leaned in closer. "Meanwhile, I have let the
Houses of Orsini and Colonna go unchecked. These two
Cardinals, once rivals, have joined forces. Burchard tells
me of plots to accuse me of simony. Force me to set aside
my sacred duty and leave Italy in disgrace."

"Cardinal Orsini and Colonna have been troublesome
since your election," Lucrezia said.

"You have heard of such treachery?" Rodrigo answered,
his interest piqued.

Lucrezia knew nothing of the sort except for the knowledge imparted by Cesare in the garden. She understood little of the political maneuvering around her but seized the opportunity to make her mark. "These Cardinals have nieces who serve the court. I always keep my ears keenly aware. They think I do not listen to mindless prattle, but I always take note."

Rodrigo stroked his chin. "And you would inform me of anything of importance?"

Lucrezia bowed her head dutifully. "Of course."

Rodrigo's face brightened with clarity. "A pilgrimage may be in order, but not to the great cathedrals. Instead, I shall journey to the Houses of both Colonna and Orsini. Travel with my glorious army, once led by your brother, as a warning and present a show of force for those who dare hinder the Vicar of Christ. Bring my auditors. Open their books. Find the taxes and assets they have kept hidden from Rome's coffers." As he spoke, his face glowed with the revenge he foretold, then his expression darkened, and he slammed the goblet down hard on the table. "It is impossible! I cannot leave my Vatican unprotected from enemies that lurk in the shadows, waiting and willing to strike in my absence!"

Lucrezia inhaled deeply, and as she exhaled, the words spilled forth. A suggestion that under any other circumstance would seem ludicrous. "Allow me to protect it, Father. A Borgia can still maintain order in your absence. The seat of Saint Peter will be safe with me. Burchard's steady hand shall guide me as he has done since I was a small girl." Of course, the thought of Burchard perched over her shoulder soured her stomach. The man held as much disdain for her as she did for him, but the idea would only work if she included her father's loyal secretary.

Rodrigo's eyes narrowed, contemplating her words. "You would be a placeholder only," he finally said sternly. "A Borgia figurehead. Decisions and conflict resolutions would be at Burchard's discretion," he continued, pointing a slender finger at her for emphasis, as he had done so many times before. A warning not to overstep her boundary of womanhood. A reminder to obey.

***

Three days had passed since Rodrigo departed to confront the disobedient Colonna and Orsini. Lucrezia busied herself in her father's apartments, mostly in his library, where his extensive collection of books was at his disposal, as were stacks, scrolls, and sealed letters waiting for his return. Not surprisingly, during her father's absence, no requests came from Cardinals eager to move forward with their interests, nor any visits or audiences with bishops, foreign dignitaries, or lords whining over taxation and land disputes. Except for Burchard, who watched over her from his small corner desk, being Pope was quite isolating and dull.

Lucrezia sat with an open book on her lap, pretending to read as her mind wove a web to escape the palace. She needed Pietra's help. "Summon my maid to bring my needlework," she said to Burchard, amused at giving the commands.

Burchard eyes narrowed and, for a moment, Lucrezia feared a scolding. "Very well," he said and sent a guard to do her bidding.

Pietra returned with a sewing basket, and as she set it before Lucrezia, she discreetly palmed the note handed to her and swiftly left.

It was late in the day when Burchard finally stood and stretched his back from an afternoon seated in his chair. He shuffled a stack of papers into a neat pile and carefully rolled them into a tight scroll before tying it tight. He tucked the parchment under his arm and turned to Lucrezia.

"Time to retire to my chamber," he told her. "I will return in the morning to escort you to Mass."

Lucrezia offered a neutral nod but smiled inwardly, wishing she could see his stern face flush with anger come morning when he found her gone.

***

The following day, Lucrezia and Pietra made their way
to one of the many palace kitchens. They carried cloaks
in satchels but were dressed as ordinary scullery maids.
Lucrezia was careful to tuck her blond curls up tight into
the white kitchen cap.

"You two," a cook with reddened cheeks and a sour face
growled, "bring water and two hens from the coop and be
quick about it! The midday stew will not make itself!"

The girls nodded hastily and hurried out the back door.
A work hand and empty wagon, one of many, waited
outside ready to be sent to the market to retrieve pantry
goods. As they approached, the wiry man in the wagon
seat frowned at them.

"What is the cook complaining about now?" he said to
Lucrezia and spat a wad of tobacco juice in the dirt. "Was
the cheese not fresh enough? Always complaining about
something, that one!" His squirrely eyes widened as he
stared at Lucrezia. "Well, girl, speak!"

Lucrezia stood frozen, unable to answer. Never had she
been addressed in such a way, and the proper response
escaped her. Failure now would mean a broken promise
to her friend. While Lucrezia's son slept comfortably in
a gilded cradle, Lorena's daughter remained missing and
separated from the person who loved her most. Yet, here
she stood, confused and helpless.

"Cook sends us to inspect all the goods," Pietra lied.
"Says the flour sacks were short of heft, and the root

vegetables were not firm enough. Nothing satisfies the old cow these days."

The man's face broke into a crooked smile, pleased with the answer. "Climb in, then, let's get on with it."

The girls obliged and sat with feet jouncing on the wagon's edge, but just outside the market, they slipped away while the driver was distracted by a slow-moving cart. Lucrezia and Pietra navigated through the bustling streets of the canal district. Ordinary people struggled with daily routines. Women argued with fishmongers, hands gesturing obscenely at the price of the day's catch. Burly men tossed dice on the street corner while vendors hawked their goods from makeshift stalls. Unsupervised children scuttled about, eyeing the bulging pockets of the wealthier class. It was a stark contrast to life within the palace walls. Squads of Vatican guards rushed by them on more than a few occasions, their heads swiveled in every direction, scrutinizing the crowd.

"They search for us," Pietra said, pulling her hood down further.

"We must be careful," Lucrezia replied. "Burchard is frantic about finding me before my father returns. If he does not, the man will surely find his head stuck on a pike."

Disguised in the thick hooded peasant cloaks pulled from their satchels, the women blended well with the hawking vendors, prostitutes, and drunken tavern patrons eager to peddle their wares or brawl in the street. The women, now on edge whenever the guards stormed by, swiftly disappeared into the tight corridors between buildings or darted behind wagons and barrels filled with grain to avoid being seen.

The potent scent of smoke and animal dung filled the chilly air, along with the polluted stench of the Tiber. Lucrezia briefly watched as the fishermen cast nets and pushed the vessels along with long wooden poles. She imagined Juan's lifeless body drifting with the slow-moving current, bloody and bloated.

Pietra touched her shoulder, breaking the unpleasant trance. "How will we find Lorena and Dominic?" she asked. "The streets grow more crowded as the day goes on, and it will be too dangerous once night falls."

Lucrezia understood Pietra's concerns, but the girl had been unusually nervous since the start of their journey. Lucrezia thought for a moment. "We may find them with the poorest of the poor. The diseased and hungry. The shunned and unfortunate ones. Do you know of such a place?"

Pietra nodded hesitantly. "I do," Pietra replied. "Come."

As they journeyed further from the bustling market center, the crowd of people dwindled. The streets became shabbier and less crowded, with beggars and sickly individuals replacing vendors and market-goers. Soon, they traveled until the road almost disappeared, and they found themselves among windowless hovels held together with little more than straw and mud. Some villagers meandered in and out of dwellings. Others crouched outside in the dirt, moaning from hunger and disease, open sores visible through tattered rags. Babes, too weak to suckle, lay motionless at the breast as outstretched arms reached for help.

As Lucrezia approached the far end of the pauper hamlet, she felt a pang of sadness in her heart. Witnessing such suffering and squalor was difficult, especially knowing the wealth and grandeur she came from. It was a stark reminder of the inequalities in the world. The church, in particular, had flourished on the backs of others, thanks to the taxes imposed on them. Her father had done nothing to improve circumstances. His campaign promises were nothing more than steps on the rung to the seat of Saint Peter. It was a shameful reality that Lucrezia could not ignore. Walking close to the small crowd gathered ahead, she wondered how anyone could survive such hardships.

Lucrezia and Pietra pushed through the villagers as their eyes scanned the area for any signs of Lorena or Dominic. Suddenly, at the center of the crowd, there stood Lorena. Lucrezia hardly recognized her friend without the novice veil that had once framed her face. Lorena was dressed in a maiden's tunic. Her dark, curly locks cascaded down her shoulders as she ladled out water to the thirsty crowd.

Dominic appeared beside her, dressed in a simple work shirt and trousers, a far cry from his usual woolen robe and hood. The women approached, relieved to have finally found them.

Seeing Lucrezia, Lorena quickly handed off the water pail and scoop to a woman beside her. She rushed to her friend with a warm embrace, and Dominic swiftly followed.

"I never thought I would see you again!" Lorena cried, giving her a hard squeeze with her thin arms.

"Nor I you," Lucrezia replied, sizing the twosome up and down. "Have you both left religious life?"

Lorena nodded. "Come," she said. "There is much to tell."

Lucrezia and Pietra followed the couple to an outdoor table with benches and a lean-to roof. Dominic kindly offered each traveler a small piece of bread, which Lucrezia and Pietra politely declined, refusing to accept food in front of the ravenous villagers who eyed it hungrily.

After escaping the abbey, four months had passed since they sat together at her mother's farm. Lucrezia was concerned about the days following Juan's death and the unknown friar who falsely testified that Juan was thrown into the river by unknown assailants, knowing it was entirely untrue. She wanted to talk to Dominic privately, but there were more important matters.

Lucrezia looked into Lorena's bottomless brown eyes, happy to finally see them. She gently held her friend's calloused hand across the table and softly asked, "Have you news of your baby?"

Lorena's face darkened, and she tightened her grip on Lucrezia's fingers, responding with a simple "no."

Dominic cleared his throat. "We traveled back to Lord Baccio's farm for news, the place of Lorena's people, but everyone was gone," he said, cutting in. "We found the farmstead in shambles and deserted, victims of the sweating disease we were told."

"Did no one survive?" Lucrezia asked, pained by the story.

"We do not know," Lorena replied.

"From there, we ministered to the poor in the district. Handing out food and clothing from aid given to us from local churches. Time after time, the donations got stolen by bandits and rogues," Dominic said, spitting on the dirt at the memory. Lorena hissed her displeasure. "My apologies," he said, touching his chest and then continued. "Our religious garb made us vulnerable to their thievery, so we found laymen's clothing."

"That is not all we found," Lorena said, smiling at Dominic. She stood and slipped her arm around his waist, and it was then that Lucrezia noticed the bulge of her stomach under her tunic. "The religious life may be over for us, but another life awaits."

Lucrezia embraced them both as Pietra remained seated. "I am happy for you both. It brings me great joy, and I pray God grants you many blessings," she said, gently touching Lorena's belly. She turned to Pietra. "Are you not pleased with the news? Come, congratulate our friends."

Dominic's eyes narrowed. "You did not tell her?" he said to Pietra, and the girl shook her head and stared at the ground. "That explains why you sit so quietly."

"It was I who found Dominic after Juan," she stammered as her voice shook, "was – gone. I told him what to tell the guards when they discovered the body."

"Why keep this from me?" Lucrezia asked. "What did it matter?"

Pietra began to sob. "I had to know my tormentor was gone. Telling you would have put you in danger had I been caught," she cried. "Forgive me for keeping this secret."

"Pietra found me," Dominic interrupted. "Told of troops searching the waterfront. She was panicked. Spreading a falsehood after what Pietra told me Juan had done was no sin to me. She was brave to have come."

"I forgive you and am grateful for your loyalty," Lucrezia said softly, taking the girl by the shoulders. It was clear the painful scars her brother left behind ran deep. "Juan will never harm you, or anyone, again."

Pietra nodded and whimpered softly.

"What will you do now?" Lucrezia asked, hoping the couple would reside in Vatican City.

"We hope to settle abroad," Lorena said, "perhaps in France. Dom has people there."

Lucrezia shifted uncomfortably. "It saddens me to hear that," Lucrezia replied. "Why not settle here? Start a farm, perhaps. I could help."

Dominic shook his head. "Staying here is no longer favorable. Corruption is too widespread," he stammered, "especially regarding the church."

"Dom, don't!" Lorena said, grasping his arm.

"She must know the truth," he replied sternly.

"Tell me," Lucrezia demanded.

"Skimming the riches from the abbeys and monasteries is no longer enough for the church. The missionaries in Rome tell of large estates taxed to the breaking point, then divided and bestowed as gifts. This is no horse trading amongst the clergy to garner favors. It is worse. Far worse, and it trickles down from the Vatican itself. I fear what happened to Lord Baccio's estate had more to do with this simony than the sweating disease..."

The words Cesare had spoken in the garden had been the truth. Greed and ambition had poisoned her father and contaminated the seat of Saint Peter.

Lorena cut Dominic's words short as she gasped loudly and pointed down the road. Out of nowhere, the sound of pounding hooves echoed through the village. A group of Vatican soldiers approached, kicking up a plume of dust in their wake, and the crowd hurriedly parted to avoid being trampled. The horses halted before them as Burchard swung down from the saddle, his face contorted with anger. Lucrezia braced herself for the man's wrath, which could be almost as terrifying as her father's.

Burchard quickly approached her, and his words would forever burn in her memory. "You must return immediately, Lucrezia. Your mother is dead."

CHAPTER FIFTEEN

Lucrezia stared dully at the familiar gardens below her bedchamber window. The cool morning air passed easily through the open shutters. She wore a thin nightgown and robe but welcomed the light breeze that embraced her. Rodrigo cooed contently in her arms, and she gazed down at the grandson Vannozza would never know. After not returning from the hay field, farmhands found Vannozza's body lifeless and cold. Some said she had recently complained of head pain and faintness, but no one knew what happened. Lucrezia tried not to think about her mother's last moments alone, but she scolded herself for not being there anyway. Fear was not something Vannozza gave in to easily, and Lucrezia prayed her mother died as she had lived.

Two days had passed since Burchard had brought Lucrezia back from the hamlet. Dominic, Lorena, and Pietra, too, had been saddled up by the soldiers and returned. One of Lucrezia's more loyal maids told of them herded into a carriage house near the stables. When asked about Burchard, the girl eagerly recounted how Burchard was now working in the bowels of the law library—a far cry from his position as Papal Secretary. Still, better than having your head on a pike, Lucrezia mused.

Lost in thought, Lucrezia did not hear the door open and close behind her but turned once the cold glare of her father bore into her. She was surprised to see him. She had expected her admonishment to come before the Council of Cardinals or, at the very least, parade her in front of the court in a dramatic show of atonement. Lucrezia placed little Rodrigo in his cradle.

Rodrigo motioned for her to sit, and she shook her head, choosing to face his wrath head-on.

"You lied," he seethed, his voice shaking with anger. You left and broke your promise to guard the seat of Saint Peter. I trusted you."

"Another promise bound me. A debt to a friend that needed repayment. An obligation more important than your precious seat. Something you will never understand."

"The girl in the carriage house."

"Yes, she and the man rescued me from the abbey. They helped me return to you," She smiled, "Is it not what you wanted?"

"You twist my words. I should execute them. Make them pay for you squandering your duty."

"You won't."

"Really? Why is that?"

Lucrezia approached her father, needing to see the depths of pain in his eyes. "Your schemes and plotting are coming to light. It is well-known that estates are absconded through excessive taxation, then divided and redistributed as you see fit. Vatican coffers overflow with ill-begotten coin. As Mother once said, nothing stays buried forever."

Rodrigo's eyes widened in surprise. Then his face broke into laughter. "You think you can stop me? You are a silly, foolish girl. A child to think you hold any relevance in the matter. What is next? Accuse me of simony, too?"

"Perhaps you are right," Lucrezia replied, unshaken by his frivolous manner. "But the trouble I cause may be great." Anger coursed through her veins. Juan's bloody specter lay before her, his life seeping out on the very floor she stood on. "You know not what I am capable of."

As her father headed towards the door, he dismissed her words with a wave. "Your wedding to Alfonso D'Este, Duke of Ferrara, has been confirmed. You will depart in two weeks. Perhaps when you spread your legs this time, you'll deliver a legitimate Borgia child. Not a bastard like the one you returned with. Now, go back to your needlework, Daughter."

"I know who killed Juan," Lucrezia suddenly said, the words spilling forth before she could stop herself.

Rodrigo stopped and turned, his face ashen. The amusement vanished. "You lie."

"He fell where you stand," she continued, strangely amused by his shock. "They may have found stab wounds on his corpse, but the poison in his veins did him in."

"Stop!" Rodrigo cried, pressing his hands to his ears.

"I had some trouble getting him down the privy," she said, careful not to mention Pietra. "But, like needlework, if you put your mind to it, much can be accomplished."

"You demon!"

"If I am a demon daughter, you are a devil father. I understand now that Satan thrives within secrets. A worm gains strength by burrowing inside pain. Inside lies. It is the truth that steals power. I confess because the truth renders you weak." The man she called father shrunk before her. "What will you do with my confession?" she continued. "Tell the Council of Cardinals? Consult canon law? Your enemies will swarm and demand your resignation. The downfall of the Borgias would be at hand. No, you will keep silent about your murderous daughter and monstrous son and keep the seat of Saint Peter. The populace deplores your excessive taxation and divisive land practices. What do you think they will do after hearing of this?"

Rodrigo stumbled to a chair and slumped down on the cushion, his face dark with concern. "What do you want?" he asked in a voice barely a whisper.

"I will give you no trouble regarding this union with D'Este. But you, dear Father, will do something for me."

Chapter Sixteen

Epilogue

As the royal carriage came to a halt, a footman opened the door and offered his gloved hand to Lucrezia as she stepped out. The sights and smells of the farm that had once belonged to her mother instantly enveloped her. Gazing around, she saw market wagons waiting to be filled with fresh produce, smelled the sweet aroma of boiling grapes, and saw bundles of drying herbs hanging from the outside kitchen beam. Even the old dog lay curled in his favorite spot near the long table where her mother once carved meat. A pang of sadness filled her heart. The one person who gave the sting of wisdom as freely as her love was missing. Lucrezia always considered Vannozza to be invincible, even from death. Now she realized death visited everyone, no matter how strong.

She quickly brushed away a tear as Lorena and Dominic approached. Arm in arm, the twosome greeted her, looking very much in love, the new owners of her mother's farm.

Lorena's belly swelled with child as her time drew near. She embraced Lucrezia warmly. "You came."

"I could not leave without saying farewell," Lucrezia said with a tightness in her throat.

Lorena grasped her shoulders. "If we are blessed with a girl, we shall name her Lucrezia," she said solemnly.

Lucrezia gently rested her hands on her friend's stomach, feeling a slight movement. "Call her Vannozza," she said, holding back the tears. "Will you do that for me?"

Lorena nodded and bowed her head. "We would be honored."

"I hear you are to be a duchess," Dominic interrupted, referring to Lucrezia's upcoming wedding.

"Duchess of Ferraro," she nodded, making a deep sweeping courtesy.

"You shall make a fine duchess, my friend," Pietra announced proudly, appearing from the outside kitchen with a small woven basket of berries and an undeniable lightness in her step. "Here," she said, passing the basket to Lucrezia. "For your journey."

"Thank you," Lucrezia said, embracing her former servant, wondering if they would meet again. Pietra's face beamed with a joyful glow, and Lucrezia hoped for nothing but happiness for the girl.

Pietra drew her close and whispered in Lucrezia's ear, "I hope the duke is sweet to you," she said in a low voice.

"As do I," Lucrezia whispered back uneasily. She forced a smile and swallowed the sadness at leaving her friends behind. "Keep me in your prayers, and I will do the same for you. If you need anything, find me. I am always here for you."

After offering her final goodbyes, Lucrezia withdrew to her carriage. She did not look back at the farm or her friends. Tucked safely in her heart, she would remember them fondly and forever. A new life was before her, a new beginning, and she knew not what it held. The footman closed and secured the door, and after a few moments, the carriage jostled down the dirt road away from the friends she loved and her mother's memory. She knew little of the Duke of Ferraro. His name was Alfonso, and he was wealthy. She was sure the marriage benefited her father. If there was no love between them, let there be at least an understanding as there was with Giovanni. She prayed he was at least kind and not cruel. There had been enough cruelty, enough brutality.

Lucrezia gazed lovingly at little Rodrigo, who sat gurgling on the nursemaid's lap and scooped up some of the berries Pietra had given her. She carelessly popped them in her mouth, savoring the sweet juice. Suddenly, her fingers touched the shape not of a plump berry but of a familiar tiny flask. Discreetly, Lucrezia slipped the bottle inside her cloak pocket and smiled. Whether the duke was kind or not, she no longer worried.

The End

Printed in Great Britain
by Amazon

43494021R00142